Debbey

Thank you for polishing up my creations and making them shine.
You are the best.

Blessings!
KC Hart

Business Smarts

&

Reckless Hearts

KC Hart

EBook ISBN: 978-1-954791-20-6

Paperback ISBN: 978-1-954791-18-3

PRAISE FOR KC'S BOOKS

Fresh Starts & Small Town Hearts

I was so impressed with KC's new book . . . *"I read it in two sittings. Her Cozy Mysteries were good, but now KC has found herself as an author and she has found her niché. Her writing seems so different . . . But in such a good way. She is a Christian romance author who is going places! Her characters are developed. I feel like I know them. They are human. They have real issues and real problems, with so much more depth than most romance stories. I found myself relating to their spiritual issues and relationship to God. KC's story will speak to many, with each seeing God's witness from their own needs. It's a MUST READ if you love flawed relationships with happy endings."* Author R Marshall Wright

A Christmas Blaze

A Pure Delight... *"This is one of the sweetest stories I've read! From tragedy to triumph, it draws you into the lives of each character. Don't miss this one!"*

Moonlight, Murder, & Small Town Secrets

"K.C. Hart knows how to grab your attention and keep you guessing."

"KC Hart tells the story with humor, wit, and the polite southern charm lacking in today's world. Keep an eye on KC Hart-she's good." Author R Marshall Wright

Music, Murder, & Small Town Romance

"If you loved Nancy Drew as a kid, you need to meet K.C. Hart!"

"A simple band competition turns into murder involving the local Casanova. This keeps you moving from one suspect to another without giving away the true villain. The dependence on God of the main character flows through the storyline in a very authentic way."

Memories, Murder, & Small Town Money

"I think this might be the best book in the series so far. The mystery is great, as usual, and kept me guessing until the end. I also really enjoyed seeing Katy's character grow and watch the sweet, honest friendship between her and Misty reach a new level. I highly recommend this book and the entire series."

"This is the most awesome series I've come across yet! I have been looking for a good Christian cozy mystery series and this is exactly what I have been searching for."

Merry Murder & Small Town Santas

"A great murder mystery that will pull you in from the beginning. So fun trying to figure out who is the killer. The author keeps the reader on a rollercoaster ride with clues and suspects. The town and characters are great fun and a little quirky. Katy is bold and gets herself into some situations that make her an excellent main character. I love reading this series and I'm looking forward to the next book. This is a clean book that doesn't have gore, but mystery and humor a plenty!"

"I loved this story, it was different. I never once gave the ending a thought, so it was a complete surprise. I love surprises! As always, the love between Katy and John was great, and the spiritual aspects were good also. The humor is always much appreciated."

Medicine, Murder & Small Town Scandal

"KC Hart gives hands and feet to a Christian way of life. KC Hart did it again. I love how her characters connect to my actual daily life. (Poor Katy, the struggle between chocolate pie and cholesterol!) I also love the way KC Hart makes belief in Jesus Christ an every day, every hour, every minute way of life, not something pulled out and shown off on "church" days or holidays.

If you need some down time, something to grab your attention and lose yourself for a few hours, get a KC Hart cozy mystery."

"Lots of twists and turns, and I had no clue "who done it" 'til the end! Loved the medical aspect too. Katy Cross keeps it interesting."

Marriage, Murder & Small Town Schemes

"You will get engulfed in this awesome Christian cozy mystery by the very talented author, KC Hart. I loved it and would highly recommend this book and the entire series."

"KC Hart doesn't disappoint with this one. This may be my new favorite!"

"I love the fact that this book has the same well developed, likable characters, along with a few new interesting ones added in... This is definitely a must read."

Mistaken Murder & Small Town Status

"Wow! Such an awesome book! I absolutely love that Christ is shared in Mistaken Murder & Small Town Status. This book kept me guessing until the very end. A definite must read. This is a great book to 'shoot the bull' about."

"Mistaken Murder & Small Town Status is a wonderful read. KC Hart has done it again with book seven of the Katy Cross Cozy Mystery series. Katy finds herself in the midst of another murder. This time it is a prize bull and the accidental death of a rancher... or was it really an accident? As the well developed plot progresses, the mystery thickens. I love how God takes a central part throughout the book. If you enjoy suspense and surprises, this is a must read."

Mistletoe, Murder &Small Town Scoundrels

"Katy Cross delivers once again! She wove family life, small town ties, and finding God's purpose into a page turner and this one kept me guessing to the end."

CHAPTER ONE

"*J*ust one more bite." Fiona held the spoon up to the old woman's pale, drooping lips. *Nana, are you even in there?* She looked into the faded blue eyes, void of emotion, or even recognition of who Fiona was or what she was doing. Fiona's heart tugged. Where was the woman who used to live in that body? "Nana." She touched the cool spoon to her grandmother's lips, coaxing her to take one more bite of the scrambled eggs. "Eat this, and I will bring you a Hershey kiss this afternoon."

Fiona dropped the spoon back onto the plastic tray. It was no use. Nana was done eating for now. She threw her thick braid of chestnut hair back over her shoulder and sighed. "It's okay," she whispered, leaning over and gently kissing her grandmother's wrinkled cheek. "It's not your fault. You're doing the best you can." Fiona pressed Nana's boney cheek against her own and blinked back tears. Not only had Nana forgotten the faces of the grandchildren she raised as her own, she had also forgotten how much she enjoyed eating. The skeletal figure in front of her was just a shadow of the plump, jovial woman who was once the rock

Fiona and her two siblings had clung to after their mother abandoned them all those years ago.

Fiona took the adult sized bib from around her grandmother's neck and glanced at the clock on the wall behind her. Ten minutes till seven. She would probably be late for work again, but she couldn't help it. Trina, the head nurse of the memory care section of the nursing home, assured Fiona that her grandmother ate twice as much for Fiona as she did for any of the nursing staff, no matter how much they tried to entice her. There was no way Fiona could make it to her grandmother's noon meal. She would be there for Nana's breakfast and dinner feedings every day. That was going to happen, no matter what. She tucked in a wayward curl that had already escaped her braid and blinked back a tear. Nana was fading away a little more every day right before her eyes.

"She ate seventy-five percent, Flo." Flo rolled the dolly over to where they sat, and Fiona handed the nursing assistant Nana's breakfast tray, tearing her eyes away from the woman who barely resembled the grandmother she loved. "I've got to run. Call if you need me."

Fiona hugged Nana's boney shoulders one more time. She stepped away from the wheelchair and hurried to the exit. Her nimble fingers punched in the passcode, keeping the Alzheimer's patients securely in the building. Snatching up a fold in her long gauzy skirt, she jogged across the parking lot to her little Volkswagen Beetle. She tossed her canvas bag in the passenger's seat and turned the key in the ignition. Fiona held her breath. The engine turned over and coughed to a start. *Thank you, Lord.* Sawyer, Fiona's brother, older by eleven months, was an ace mechanic. His willingness to tinker with her vehicle and scavenger used replacement parts as needed was the only reason she had a car that would run.

Fiona absolutely loathed the way their backyard looked

like a junkyard, with old car parts scattered hither and yonder. There were always at least three vehicles in different stages of repair that she had to push the mower around.

She shouldn't complain, not really. Sawyer's side business of buying wrecked cars, fixing them, and reselling them, helped pay the bills. One day soon, he planned on opening his own auto body/mechanic shop, but he had to keep dipping into his savings to pay for things like a broken stove, or their little sister's trip to the dentist. No, her car needed fixing, but she would not bother Sawyer as long as it would get her from point A to point B.

The little car sputtered into the parking lot behind the coffee shop. She killed the engine, and the Beetle sighed, relieved it survived the trip. Fiona's gray eyes scanned the lot. *Oh, man.* Gary Denton's truck was already there. Gary, her boss, was aware she stopped by and fed her grandmother every morning, but until last week, he didn't know that she was sometimes ten or fifteen minutes late starting her shift.

Thank goodness for Sarah. She clocked Fiona in on days she was running late. Fiona always made sure she stayed an additional ten or fifteen minutes after clocking out in the afternoon, or worked through part of her lunch break, so she was not actually stealing the wages. That; however, didn't matter to Gary. He had dropped in last week at 7:00. She hadn't gotten there until 7:10, but was miraculously already clocked in. No one would tell Gary who had punched the time clock for her. He immediately put her on probation, along with the other two employees who refused to rat her out. Her behind was already on the line.

This day was not starting off well. Fiona pushed open the back door of Bayou Bean and stumbled through the doorway. She glanced down at the untied shoestring of her white Converse, then back to the time clock where Gary stood.

"Pete called in." Gary looked down over the top of his

black horn-rimmed glasses sitting on the tip of his pointed nose. Even though his five foot nine inch frame was only two inches taller than Fiona, his icy stare always made her feel small. "I need you to help Sarah at the counter."

"Uh." Fiona glanced toward the time clock. "Yes, sir. Let me just clock in."

Gary stepped to the side and waved his hand in front of him. "By all means. Please do."

Fiona grabbed her card from the metal tray on the wall and quickly punched in. Gary turned and headed toward the tiny kitchen area where she preferred to work. She grabbed a dark brown canvas apron from the peg nearby and slipped it over her head. *Lord, you know I have to feed Nana, and I need this job. Please make Gary go light on me.* She tied the strings of her apron around her narrow waist and gave them an extra hard tug. It would take a miracle to keep Gary off her back today, that was for sure.

Fiona stepped into the front of the brightly lit coffee house. She inhaled the revitalizing aroma of freshly ground beans that appropriately filled the shop. The whirring of the espresso machine blended with the chatter of the customers in the busy, little shop.

Sarah looked over her shoulder and spied Fiona. A bright smile flashed on her face. Fiona hurried to the counter, a twinge of guilt stinging her gut. She forced a cheery smile in place and looked back at her friend. *Why did I ever put Sarah in this predicament? These are my problems, not hers.*

"Gary has been breathing down our necks all morning," Sarah whispered, stepping up to where Fiona started taking the order from a blond-headed man in a tee-shirt and jeans.

The guy was a regular, so Fiona had already started ringing him up before he spoke. Sarah knew almost all the regulars by name. Of course, Sarah, being Sarah, had learned everything about everyone she ever met within the first five minutes of meeting them. Fiona was not shy, but she did not find it necessary to delve into the inner workings of the past of every person she encountered at Bayou Bean the way her friend did. Dealing with her own life occupied too many of her thoughts lately. She did know what most of the regulars ordered. Learning those tidbits of information made her life run a little smoother.

"He met me at the time clock." Fiona handed the man across the counter his receipt and turned to her friend. "Look, I am really sorry I got you involved in my mess." She looked at the room full of people sitting at the little tables sipping their drinks or standing in line waiting to be served. "You got slammed this morning."

"It's no problem." Sarah reached her arm around Fiona's shoulders and gave a quick squeeze. "It just got this way. I promise. Besides, you would do the same for me." Sarah looked behind her where Gary stood in the doorway, his lips squeezed together in a thin line. "We better get to hopping. The dragon is going to start breathing fire out his nose and light this place up if he sees us actually being nice to each other."

Fiona glanced over her shoulder at Gary, then tugged on the bottom of her pale pink tee-shirt. She could talk to Gary after the rush of customers slowed down. Her hours were 7:00 to 2:00, but if she explained her situation to him again, maybe he would let her come in at 7:30, or even 8:00, and work later. She pulled a deep breath in through her nose and turned back to the next customer. She had to figure something out. It wasn't fair to Sarah to keep making her work short-handed, even if she acted like it was no big deal.

CHAPTER TWO

*T*he week was not going well. Langston Wade pulled his gleaming, black truck into a parking space behind his office. A potential client was coming in at 9:00 to discuss building a new strip mall on the other side of town. He glanced at the clock on the dashboard...7:45 am. His secretary usually arrived at 8:30. There was time to walk down to Bayou Bean, grab a muffin, and a to-go cup of his favorite coffee.

All the paperwork should be in place before this client arrived. If not, their company did not look professional. That would not happen. Langston never let that happen. He reviewed a lot of the specs and plans earlier in the week, but there were still a few loose ends to tie up. Lucas, Langston's little brother who would actually oversee the construction, would be at the meeting as well. It was Langston's job; however, to make sure their numbers for the cost of the project were exact. They were accurate, but after last night, he needed to sit down and go over everything one more time. Doing business always settled him down, cleared his mind. Numbers made sense. Numbers never did the unexpected. Numbers were not like women.

Langston stepped out of his truck and adjusted his charcoal gray tie. He reached over and straightened his suit coat laying in the passenger's seat. No need to put it on until he got back to his air-conditioned office. Lucas would show up at the meeting in his usual jeans and a tee-shirt, but his brother did not understand why dressing for business was important. Langston had explained this to his little brother a thousand times. The power behind strong impressions was key. A man wearing a suit drove home the idea of security to their customers. It was a mind game, but it worked. Will Smith and Tommy Lee Jones wore suits on *Men In Black.* Adam Cartwright, the smart, brooding son on *Bonanza,* wore the black shirts, but Little Joe, the carefree son, wore the brighter colors.

Lucas had listened, but Langston's words went in one ear and out the other. Lucas said their reputation would speak for itself, and it did to a certain point. When clients were paying hundreds of thousands of dollars, even millions to get a project done, they needed to see someone who looked like they were used to dealing with that type of responsibility.

Langston crossed the street and hurried the couple of blocks to Bayou Bean. There wasn't a single parking spot in the area. Good thing he hadn't wasted his time driving here. Gary Denton was not Langston's favorite person, but the man hit a stroke of genius when he opened the coffeehouse in the business district. Langston's brown eyes scanned the rows of cars up and down the street, looking for the steel colored Miata Danika Hawthorn owned. He didn't see her car. Good. Since their break up last month, he avoided her like the plague.

"Good morning, ladies." Langston smiled and held the door open for a couple of middle-aged women walking out of Bayou Bean. "Beautiful morning, isn't it?" He stepped inside and sniffed the pleasant aroma of brewing coffee. A few people stood in front of him in the line, but the morning rush hour looked like it was over. He would be back in plenty of time.

Langston dropped his hand into his pants pocket and fumbled with his keys. Most everyone in the coffee house gathered in groups of twos or threes. That was fine, but being alone was fine, too. He had nothing against dating. He and Danika had gone out like clockwork every Saturday night for over a year. The clockwork thing, though, that was part of the problem.

He had not dated anyone in over a month. Not since the break-up date with Danika Hawthorn. They were a lot alike, him and Danika. She worked for the mayor, was the youngest member of the city council, and excelled in her work environment. She was a master at organizing any situation and getting the expected outcome. The problem was, he was not a situation. He *would not* allow her to put him in her day planner like a task she could check off her list.

"Langston, fourteen months is long enough for casual dating. We've had enough time to get to know each other, to establish a solid relationship, but it's time to move it to the next level."

The next level. Like getting engaged was some sort of business venture. Sure, spending time with Danika was what? Not fun. Comfortable maybe? She was smart, could hold her own on almost any topic, including college football and deer hunting, but he didn't get engaged to a woman because she looked great in a dress and could shoot a rifle.

"Danika, marriage is a lifelong commitment. We can't get engaged because it fits into your schedule." The look on her face when he told her he had no plans to get married in the near future had not been pretty. Shock, agitation, determination all flashed through those ice-blue eyes. Everything but hurt. Langston's brow furrowed. He shuffled forward in the line, staring at the beverage list behind the counter. Had Danika ever shown true hurt . . . or genuine joy over the past fourteen months? If she had, she kept it reigned in so tight that he had not seen it.

"Hey, Langston. Do you want your usual?"

Langston looked over the list of beverages written on an enormous chalkboard behind the counter. "Hey, Sarah. Yeah, give me the usual, extra hot, and do you have any blueberry muffins left?"

"We sure do. Have a seat and I'll get it out to you in a second." Sarah's dimples shined in her cheeks. "Love that tie, by the way."

See, she looks genuinely happy. Danika never just looked happy; everything was rehearsed. Langston ran his debit card through the scanner, paying for the coffee and muffin, and leaving Sarah a generous tip. He walked over to a little table near the front window and sat in the wooden chair. *I wasn't sad about the break-up either. Not really.*

Langston looked out the window and across the street. A man and woman, probably his age, walked down the sidewalk chatting and laughing. He and Danika had never acted like that. The fourteen months they dated were more like business meetings. Nice, cordial, but not what a date should have been like.

"Langston, look. You're thirty and I'm thirty-one. We are not children, and honestly, we both know that we make the perfect couple. If you are determined to keep playing this game of the unattainable bachelor, though, I need to move on. It's time to fish or cut bait."

The corner of Langston's mouth crept up into a smile at the memory. "If that's the way you want it, then okay."

"Great!" Danika's nude lips had stretched into a smile,

showing her full set of perfectly capped teeth. "I already have the ring picked out."

"No, you misunderstood me." Danika's blue eyes had stretched wide, then shot out daggers before returning to her controlled self. "Consider yourself set free, Danika. I'm not going to marry you."

What would his life be like now if he had said yes? A shudder ran across the back of his neck. He never should have allowed that relationship to drag on as long as it had. Being alone had its merits. He reached over and pulled a napkin from the silver holder. He was doing fine on his own.

His phone vibrated in his pocket, pulling him back to the present. He pulled it out and looked at the number. His housekeeper. "Good morning, Mrs. Butler. How was your weekend?"

"Oh, that's' not good." Langston flopped back in the little wooden chair, legs splayed in front of him. "No, ma'am. You go ahead and go. I will be fine." Langston stared up at the ceiling, one arm dangling beside him. The older woman's voice continued to rattle from the phone. "No, ma'am, I would never expect you to stay here with me if your family needs you. She's fortunate she only broke her leg. Falling from that high on a ladder could have been a lot worse. Yes, ma'am, twins are a handful and a blessing. Of course, you should go help your daughter. I would expect nothing less from you. Yes, ma'am, just leave the house keys at my office when you head out of town."

Great, breaking up with a girlfriend was one thing, but losing his housekeeper was a completely different can of beans. Langston sat back up in the little chair and straightened his tie. The three old women a couple of tables over stared, eyes stretched wide like owls. He smiled and nodded. They smiled in return and slowly turned back to whatever bit of gossip they were analyzing with their bran muffins and lattes.

He looked around the rest of the coffee shop sheepishly. No one seemed to be paying him any attention. Good. He looked back toward the counter. Shouldn't Sarah be bringing his coffee? Another woman, taller than Sarah, wiped the countertop. The woman stared out toward the front window as her slender arm made circular motions along the countertop with the cloth. The woman reminded Langston of something. A parrot? No, a parrot was too brightly colored. Under the coffee-colored apron all the Bayou Bean workers wore, she was dressed in a pale pink tee-shirt that fit her curves nicely. He glimpsed of a bit of a pastel skirt hanging on her narrow hips as she turned to the side. No, not a parrot, but some sort of exotic bird caught in a cage, longing to be out from behind the counter and free to do whatever she was daydreaming about. He watched her work her way down the counter, her body moving in a natural rhythm, her eyes gazing out into the unknown . . . until they stopped on him. Her eyes, a dark gray, like a rain cloud right before the downpour starts, suddenly zeroed in on Langston's face, focusing on her. He glanced away, heat creeping up his neck.

His phone buzzed again, and he looked down, thankful for the distraction. A picture of Danika Hawkins appeared on the screen. *Nope, not today, swim away little shark. You are free of me.*

CHAPTER THREE

"*T*ake this order to Mr. Wade."

"Hmm?" Fiona blinked, clearing the cobwebs from her brain. "Mr. Wade?"

"Yes." Gary pushed the tray toward her again, raising his eyebrows. "The guy by the window in the white shirt and charcoal gray tie, Langston Wade. Do you think you can take him his order?"

"Sorry." Fiona's cheeks blushed pink. She dropped the wiping cloth under the counter out of sight and took the tray from Gary's hands. "Yes, sir. No problem."

Langston Wade. Was this the guy that Sarah was always gushing about, calling a Greek statue? The man looked up and ran his fingers through his wavy blond hair. Yeah, he did kind of look like he belonged on a movie screen or a cologne bottle or something. No wonder Sarah always made sure she took his order.

Where was Sarah, anyway? Fiona looked down the counter, then around the shop, sure her friend would want to deliver the man's coffee. Ah, there she was, stuck in the middle of the three old chatterboxes that came in every morning like clockwork to drink coffee and gossip about all the latest happenings around town. Fiona willed Sarah to turn around, but Sarah continued to chat with the women, not getting Fiona's telepathic nod. She, on the other hand, sensed Gary's beady eyes boring a hole into the back of her head like a power drill.

Fiona straightened her shoulders and started around the counter to where Mr. Greek god sat, looking a little on the melancholy side. What could a man who looked like that, dressed in clothes that probably cost more than her car, possibly be sad about? Fiona held the tray up high, weaving around the crowded dining floor between chairs and customers as she neared Langston Wade.

It was an out-of-body experience. She felt the coffee flying off the tray. Her foot tangled in her shoestring, then her skirt, then her other foot. She tumbled toward him, silently praying she would face plant the floor and not his lap, that the coffee would hit one of the nearby old men in the coveralls and not the Greek statue dressed in a starched white shirt and charcoal gray silk tie. But... sometimes life was cruel.

Fiona's body hurdled downward. The extra-large, extra hot cup of coffee collided with the man's pristine shirt, the contents pouring down the front of his chest. She looked up, searching for his face, but the fall continued out of her control. Her head collided with his knee, slipping off as he stood from his chair, effectively landing her on the floor at his feet.

"Hot! Hot! Hot!" Langston Wade bolted upward, yelling the words at the top of his lungs. A few drops of the coffee splattered against the back of Fiona's neck as she practically groveled at the man's feet. He was right. It was definitely hot, hot, hot. Could he press charges like that woman at McDonald's had done years ago? Assault with a deadly beverage?

Fiona untangled her legs from her skirt and shoestrings while Langston Wade panted like a pregnant woman giving birth to twins. His face was just as red and as intense as the women in labor on that show *Call The Midwife,* the one her grandmother used to love to watch. For a second Fiona almost yelled for him to push, but caught herself before the words escaped her lips. "I am so, so sorry." She pulled a handful of paper napkins from the metal holder on the table and began dabbing uselessly at his stained shirt, but that shoestring, that skirt, fouled her up a second time. She tumbled forward, plowing into his chest.

The Greek god swayed backwards against the wooden chair behind him, both of them spiraling out of control. He grabbed for something—*anything*—to stop their fall, but all he found was her shoulders. They both landed on the floor in front of the picture window, giving Old Man Humphrey a perfect view of the whole kerfuffle. The geriatric grouch shook his finger at Fiona. He'd probably give her an earful when he came in later for his usual bran muffin and black coffee.

Fiona swallowed, not daring to breathe, her nose a mere inch from Langston's nose. She stared into his brown eyes. The heat of the coffee warmed the front of her chest as well, and oddly enough, it pulsed through her shoulders and neck–practically her entire body. "I really am sorry."

"Don't move," Langston hissed through clamped teeth.

"I was just trying to . . ."

"Don't move." The vein on the side of his temple pulsed, his words a little louder. His eyes glared into Fiona's. "Your help is going to put me in the hospital."

"I . . ." Fiona's words died on her lips. The man's eyes narrowed. She held still, and he lifted her up and rolled to the side. She watched him stand. What should she do now? Sirens wailed somewhere in the distance, drawing closer.

Was there a fire nearby? She was definitely a little warm. Langston Wade held out his hand. Fiona stared at it, then up at his face with a deer in the headlights look. He nodded, eyebrows arched. She slipped her hand into his, and he catapulted her upward, none too gently.

Langston's gaze lingered on Fiona for a moment longer before turning away. She slowly looked at the rest of the people in the coffee shop. Every face stared back, eyes stretched wide, no words coming from anyone's mouths, even the three old birds who lived to gossip.

"Who called an ambulance?" Langston Wade's voice bellowed out through the silence like an angry lion, unhappy with the prey he had just devoured.

"I did." Gary stepped around the counter, twisting the wet dishcloth in his hands. "I think we need to make sure you are not burned or injured, Mr. Wade . . . Langston."

"I'm fine," Langston snapped, not quite as loud. "Go tell them to leave."

Fiona bit her bottom lip, suppressing a smile as Gary scurried out the front door to do Langston's bidding. This was, beyond a shadow of a doubt, her last day of employment at Bayou Bean, and all of this was almost worth it to see someone give Gary a taste of his own medicine. *Almost.*

"Is there a back door out of here?" Langston Wade asked.

"Hmm?" Fiona looked from Gary's retreating back to sodden, wrinkled Langston Wade.

"Is there another way out of this place besides the front door?" Langston repeated the question, slower this time, as if talking to a child.

"Oh, uh, yeah. You wanna sneak out the back?" Fiona looked up at Langston. He had to be at least six foot two. "Follow me."

"No." Langston's eyes narrowed. "Well . . . yes. Wait." He

put a hand on Fiona's arm, then pulled it away. "Tie your shoe first."

"Good idea," Fiona said. Langston righted the chair that had tripped him up. Fiona put her foot in the seat and tied her shoe. "I really am sorry about this, Mr. Wade. I'm not normally a clumsy person."

Langston looked over her shoulder, out the window where the crowd was growing. Gary helplessly tried to block the entrance of the ambulance crew. "Just get me out the back door, and we will forget this ever happened."

"Right." Fiona dropped her foot back to the floor and hitched up her skirt, careful to make sure it was not tangling her feet. "Follow me."

Fiona weaved through the chairs, ignoring the people at the other tables who continued to stare, none daring to speak. They went behind the counter and through the rear hallway to the back door. "Uh, do you want me to grab you another coffee for the road?"

"No." Langston paused in the doorway, pulling the soppy white dress shirt from his pants. He unbuttoned the buttons, revealing a coffee stained tee-shirt underneath. "What's your name?"

"Fiona." Fiona's eyes traveled from the man's hands up to his face. "Fiona Madison."

"Well, Fiona Madison. After today, I may never drink coffee again."

Langston Wade turned and walked across the little parking lot, pulling off the stained shirt and tossing it in the green dumpster as he passed.

"You okay?"

"What?" Fiona turned.

"Are you okay?" Sarah asked again, walking up behind her. Sarah stared across the parking lot at Langston Wade's

disappearing form as he hurried down the alleyway. "You fell
. . . twice."

"I'm fine."

"What did he smell like?"

"What?" Fiona stared down at her friend.

"What did he smell like? A guy that looks like that, and
dresses like that . . . he has to smell heavenly."

"Sarah." Fiona let out a sigh and shook her head. "You are
hopeless." She waited, but Sarah continued to stare, wanting
an answer. "He smelled like coffee. Scalding hot black coffee."

CHAPTER FOUR

*L*angston pulled his tee-shirt over his head and tossed it in the back of his truck. The secretary had parked in her usual spot behind their office building, but Lucas's old beat up truck wasn't on the lot. He pulled his phone from his pant pocket and climbed behind the wheel. 8:30. He had only been gone an hour, but it seemed like ten hours. Still, if he drove home and changed, he would be late for the meeting. He pulled in a breath of air and blew it out in a huff. Of all the days to have coffee poured all over him. No, there was never a good day to have coffee poured all over him.

He punched Lucas's number in the phone, started his truck, and waited for him to answer. There was no way around it. He had to go home, shower, and change. Mrs. Butler kept his shirts ironed and ready in his closet, along with his freshly dry-cleaned suits. He could be at his house in ten minutes, shower and change in fifteen, and be back in ten. He would be late, but not ridiculously late.

"Where are you?" Langston barked. "I ran into a snag and need you to start this meeting without me."

"I'm almost at the office. I heard you got burned at Bayou Bean. What happened?"

"A barista poured scalding hot coffee down my shirt. That's what happened." Langston pushed the gas pedal, moving faster. He passed the Carson Bayou City Limits sign heading to his house a couple of miles out of town. "Then she fell on top of me just before Gary Denton, the owner, called an ambulance." Laughter floated from the other end of the phone, and Langston rolled his eyes. "Look, get to the office, set the man up in the boardroom and offer him . . . coffee." Lucas chuckled a little more. "I should be back no later than 9:15."

"I'm sorry, brother. But you have to admit, it does sound kind of funny. What did you do to make Sarah pour coffee on you?"

"It wasn't Sarah. It was a woman named Fiona Madison. I've seen her in there, but she never waits on me." Langston reached over and flipped up the air conditioner, pointing the vent toward his neck and face. "She's tall, gray-blue eyes, brown curly hair."

"Yeah, I know who she is. She's kind of quiet. What did you do to her?" Lucas asked, amusement dripping from his voice.

"Nothing," Langston snapped, pulling up to a stop sign. "She tripped. Her shoe was untied, and she was wearing a long skirt. Gary needs to make the girls wear something to work that they can actually work in."

"Bro, I hope you didn't tell her that."

"I didn't tell the woman anything. I let her dump scalding hot coffee on me and fall on me like a sack of potatoes." Langston slowed his truck and pulled into his long paved driveway. "As soon as I got her off me, I hightailed it out of the place. I'm sure I will be the topic of everybody's conversation at church on Sunday. The Hampton sisters and Mrs.

Clark were there for their morning chat. I imagine they couldn't wait to spread it around that I bellowed like a bull before falling down, taking the waitress with me."

"Poor girl. I hope you didn't scare her half to death."

"Poor girl?" Langston parked his truck in front of the modern sprawling two-story house. The pale gray brick next to the black roof with multiple gables and narrow rectangular windows made the house feel like it belonged next to a beach on the West coast, not in the countryside of Carson's Bayou. "Believe me, I'm the one you should feel sorry for. That *poor girl* probably laughed her head off after I left."

Langston ended the call and headed upstairs to hop in the shower. He looked in the bathroom mirror at the red splotches on his chest. There were no blisters. He would get Mrs. Butler to get him some aloe vera gel. He stepped into the stream of hot water and closed his eyes. The water hit his shoulders. No, Mrs. Butler was gone. He would keep an eye on the burns. If they started to blister, he would call his doctor, but it was already feeling close to normal. It didn't look like it actually burned the skin.

He picked up the shampoo and squirted a small amount in his palm, quickly lathering and rinsing his hair and body. He remembered the poor woman staring into his face like a frightened doe, and the corner of his mouth pushed up into a small smile. He had done a lot of yelling and glaring. Yeah, he probably needed to drop back by the coffee shop and offer to buy everybody a cup of coffee or something. Gary was probably laying a duck, worried that he was going to sue him.

His attitude was much improved by the time Langston was dressed and driving back to his office. He would not go back to Bayou Bean today, but he would stop in tomorrow. Fiona Madison had not really harmed anything but his pride. He would show them all that he could be a good sport about the whole thing. He did think the woman should rethink her work attire with her gypsy skirt and Converse tennis shoes. She was pretty in a wild sort of way, but nobody wanted a gypsy serving their coffee. Especially a gypsy who couldn't keep her shoes tied.

"I can't believe he's firing you." Sarah looked over her shoulder at the little kitchen area where Gary was working. "I have half a mind to quit, too."

"Don't be ridiculous." Fiona looked at Sarah, an affectionate smile on her face. "You love working here, and Gary is good about working around your class schedule." She leaned over and pulled the industrial mop, heavy with pine scented water from the bucket, and turned the crank to remove the excess water. "I don't fit in. This fiasco." Fiona nodded her head to where she had spilled the coffee earlier. "It simply sealed the deal. Gary was getting ready to fire me anyway." Fiona lifted the mop from the bucket and flopped it to the floor. Sarah's friendship was a treasure, but she had no clue what losing this job would mean to Fiona, and she wanted to keep it that way.

Working at the Bayou Bean and cleaning a couple of houses every week, getting as many hours as possible to pay the bills, was something Sarah wouldn't understand. Fiona glanced over at Sarah's cute, manicured hands. Her friend went every week with her mom to get her nails done and eat lunch at the Gumbo Hut. That was part of her normal life. If Sawyer couldn't come up with the money difference because she didn't have this job, she wasn't sure how they would keep the lights on and put food on the table. She sighed and slung her braid over her shoulder. That was her normal life. Then there was Callie, with all her school activities. No, Sarah didn't need to hear all that.

Sarah left her to go wait on a customer, and Fiona pushed the mop back and forth across the floor. At least Gary was letting her finish out the day. Tomorrow she would look for another job. Not waitressing. Well, not unless push came to shove. She could probably get on at the Gumbo Hut. Maybe not if they found out she spilled coffee all over a customer and her boss had to call an ambulance.

The mop slapped against the ceramic tile floor, taking some of Fiona's frustrations away with the work. Why had she been so stupid? She graduated from high school with top grades and a partial scholarship to the local college. College had been her key to a better life, not only for her, but for Callie, Sawyer, and even Nana, but she had thrown it all away. All for Jeff Peterson and his stupid marriage proposal.

Like an idiot, she dropped out of all her classes in the second semester of her freshman year. Jeff said he wanted to get married. He was working offshore. There was no need for her to continue with school. He promised he would support them both. Even now, thinking about how dumb she had been made her stomach queasy.

Jeff left for his thirty-day hitch, and she dropped her classes so she could get everything done. She was supposed to find them a place to live, and when Jeff got back in, they would tie the knot. The only problem was, three days before he came off his hitch, his mother called and told her about Amy West, the girl that lived next door. The girl who was pregnant with Jeff's child. Jeff denied it at first, of course, but after a few days, people couldn't help but talk.

"Jeff is seeing his next door neighbor on the side," the mail lady said, shaking her head. "I heard he's been seeing both of you for at least three months."

Fiona had gone to the college to see if she could pick back up her classes. They assured her she could, but the scholarship would no longer apply.

"Okay Fi, get off the couch and get a shower." Nana said two weeks later. "Feeling sorry for yourself will not get anything done. Get yourself together, and go get yourself a job."

"You don't understand, Nana." Fiona continued pushing the mop, remembering how Nana had hugged her and given her a dose of tough love.

"Fi, life has dealt you a blow," Nana said, sitting beside her that morning, "but sitting on the couch all day wishing things were different will not change a thing. If you want to go to college, go to work and make it happen."

Fiona eventually found a job at the grocery store and started putting a little money back. The plan was to earn enough money to take a few college classes in the evening. She would work and go to school part time until she got what she wanted. That plan had fallen through, too. Nana's memory made it dangerous for her to be at home alone. Someone had to stay with her.

Stupid, stupid, stupid. Now here you are, no job, and no job prospects. Fiona picked the mop up and dropped it back in the bucket, standing for just a minute with her eyes closed, needing to regain her composure before returning to the counter.

A picture of Langston Wade bellowing the words "hot, hot, hot" popped into her head. Her face broke into a smile, despite the sadness in her eyes. Poor guy. Hopefully, the coffee had not actually burned his skin. He was probably a decent fellow when he wasn't being set on fire with his beverage of choice. It was so nice to watch Gary squirm when Langston asked who had called an ambulance.

She wiped the back of her hand across her damp forehead

and pushed the mop bucket back to the hallway at the back of the building. Langston Wade was a snob. That was obvious. The way he tossed that expensive looking shirt in the trash without even attempting to get out the coffee stain said a lot about the man. He was used to having things his way, perfectly done, with no messing around. Sarah said the man had more money than dirt to go along with his looks. Hopefully, he would do like he had said and forget about the whole coffee spilling incident. The last thing she needed was to be brought up on some kind of assault charges by one of Carson's Bayou's golden boys.

No, if Langston Wade would simply forget about her, she would certainly forget about him.

CHAPTER FIVE

*L*angston reached both arms out from his chest and stretched, pulling in a long breath of air. Today was a great day. He could feel it. When he got back to the office yesterday morning around 9:20, the client had not arrived. The man had phoned their office and said he was running a few minutes late. At 9:30, their meeting started, and everything had gone off without a hitch.

After work, Lucas had invited him to eat a home cooked dinner with him and his new wife Vivian. Apparently, Langston's side show in front of the coffee shop window had been quite entertaining for several of the people in the business district. The group that had gathered outside the window during the coffee spill had quickly spread the word of his humiliation around town.

"It's kind of sad that a man getting coffee dumped on his shirt is the hot topic of conversation on everyone's lips," Vivian said, setting a plate of baked pork chops in front of him. She sat down next to Lucas and across from Langston. "But Linda at the bank said you were being described as a bull in a china shop."

Langston was a little perturbed to be the topic of conversation around town. Eating a great meal, and then enjoying the evening with his brother and sister-in-law, had helped his outlook on the whole situation tremendously. Something new would happen soon and people would forget about his little show and move on to talk about something else.

He was running late today. Even though he hated tardiness, he refused to let the problems he found while getting ready for work ruin his mood. This morning, when he got out of the shower and stepped on the dirty towel and clothes he had taken off the day before, the realization hit him he needed to get on the ball and find a housekeeper. He had sort of taken for granted over the past few years that someone picked up his dirty clothes from the bathroom floor every day and took them where they needed to be. He hadn't done a load of laundry since college. Next, there was the problem of breakfast. Bacon was not frying when he came down the stairs to get the paper from the steps. He could make it without a live-in housekeeper, obviously. He was, after all, a grown man, but he did need someone to help keep the place up until Mrs. Butler came back, whenever that was. He would get his secretary to look for someone today.

Langston glanced at his watch. 9:00. There was time to run over to Bayou Bean and set things right with that waitress, then go to the office. He was late anyway. Might as well eat his humble pie and get it behind him.

"Good morning."

Langston walked up to the counter and smiled down at Sarah's beaming face. A couple of women dressed for work passed by with their coffees in hand and nodded in his direction. Good. He missed the early morning rush. This would be a lot easier without a room full of customers listening in. "Good morning, Sarah. Is Gary and the rest of the employees around?"

Sarah's smile melted away like butter from steaming hot corn on the cob. "Uh, yeah," she stammered. "Just a second." She turned and stepped through the little doorway to the back, quickly returning with Gary and a pimple-faced teenage boy.

"Langston, can I fix you your usual, on the house of course," Gary said, wiping his hands on a dish towel.

Langston looked past Gary, waiting for Fiona to walk out of the kitchen area. "That would be great, Gary. I wanted to let you know I am fine, and no harm was done." Gary swallowed and a nervous smile appeared on his face. "As a matter of fact," Langston continued, "I want to buy everybody a coffee and a muffin, or whatever they want to let them know that there are no hard feelings about yesterday."

"That's completely unnecessary," Gary said, relief washing over his face. "Your reaction was probably just a normal reaction. Of course, that is only a guess, since our staff aren't in the habit of spilling coffee on people."

"Of course." Langston raised an eyebrow, watching Gary squirm under his gaze. "But I want to do it anyway, so ring it all up, please." He waited as Sarah rang up the three orders, but Fiona still did not appear from the back. Maybe she was off today. He watched Gary and the teen disappear into the back to make the coffees. Sarah stepped to the glass case connected to the counter and pulled out a cream filled pastry. "Where's the other waitress? I wanted to get her something, too."

Sarah straightened up from the case and sat her cream puff on the counter. She glanced over her shoulder, leaning forward. "Gary sacked her yesterday," she whispered, eyes stretched wide. "He let her finish the day, then paid her and sent her home."

"That's too bad." Langston's mouth drew into a flat line, and he stared at the doorway leading to the kitchen area. "I should have known Gary would do that." He cut his eyes back to Sarah, who continued to watch him. "Do you know her phone number?"

"Yes." Sarah pulled her phone from her apron pocket. She pulled up Fiona's number and repeated it to Langston. "You want me to write it down for you?"

"No." Langston smiled politely. "I've got it. How much do I owe you for the coffee and, uh, stuff?"

Langston paid the tab, dropped a tip in the jar, and left the coffee shop, forgetting the coffee Gary was making for him. He should have come by yesterday, before Gary had a chance to let the girl go. He could put a little pressure on the man, and he would probably give the woman her job back. Was that the right way to handle this? Probably not. Gary, being Gary, would resent rehiring the waitress and would, no doubt, make things hard on her. He hurried down the sidewalk back to his office building. His phone buzzed, and he reached into his pocket. A text from Mrs. Butler appeared on the screen reminding him to pick up his dry-cleaning this afternoon and that Lester had an appointment with the groomer at the end of the week. He texted back a thank you and slipped the phone back in his pocket.

He didn't even know what cleaner his clothes were at or what groomer his English Mastiff used. He would have to call Mrs. Butler at lunch and find out. He stopped by his truck and retrieved his suit coat, then hurried into his office.

"I was beginning to think you were taking a sick day after your little injury yesterday." Mrs. Dean looked down her nose over her thin rectangular glasses as Langston stepped up to her desk. "You seem to be in one piece, I guess."

"I'm fine, but I have a problem. Mrs. Butler is going to be out of town for a while. I don't need another live-in house-keeper while she's gone, but I need somebody to pick up things and run some errands for me. Is there a place around here that offers that kind of thing?"

"Not a business, no." Mrs. Dean tapped her puckered lips. A mischievous glint entered her eyes. "But I can get in touch with the woman who cleans the mayor's house. The mayor's wife says she does a wonderful job. I've thought about contacting her to help with my house, but I've never gotten around to it. Want me to give her a call to come in for an interview?"

"Yes, that would be good." Langston picked up the morning mail from the corner of Mrs. Dean's desk and headed to his office. He hung his suit coat in the closet and sat down behind his desk. He pulled out his cell phone and punched in the number for Fiona Madison, but stared at the number. What would he say to the woman if he actually made the call? *I'm sorry you got fired when you dumped hot coffee all over me.* No, that didn't sound right. He couldn't send her flowers or a gift. That wasn't appropriate in this situation. Even if it was, he didn't have her address. The intercom buzzed, and he sighed and set his phone on his desk. "Yes?"

"The new cleaning lady will be in at two to talk about the job."

"Okay. Thank you."

Langston leaned back in his leather office chair and picked back up the stack of mail. No, he had better just leave the whole Fiona Madison thing alone. He had made peace as best he could with Bayou Bean. It was time to let everyone forget about his little spill, including him.

CHAPTER SIX

*F*iona tugged again on the black pencil skirt. She had borrowed it from her little sister for the job interview, but it looked like that was a mistake. She and Callie weighed the same, but her little sister was a good four inches shorter than her five-foot seven frame. Callie's skirt did not want to stay where it was supposed to, and trying to keep the thing knee length instead of a miniskirt that went up to her ribcage was turning into a constant battle.

As a kid, her brother always made fun of her knobby knees. Even now, she hated wearing skirts that didn't come to her ankles. She pulled into the Wade Brothers parking lot and swung her legs from her car. She ran her palm down the front of her calves. Smooth. Good. The dry shave a couple of hours ago had left a faint rash on a few spots on her shins, but it couldn't be helped. The call to come in for the interview did not give her much time to get ready. She had slathered her skin with baby lotion and hoped for the best.

Maxi skirts were definitely easier, but the loose fitting, free flowing garments she loved so much didn't scream efficient, competent secretary or filer, or receptionist, or whatever this position was for. She stood in the space between her open car door and car frame and drug the skirt back down in its proper place again. She ran her hands over the baby blue sweater, smoothing out the wrinkles. She bent down and looked in the side mirror. No yellow or brown splotches stuck in her teeth from the Butterfinger she ate at lunch.

"Okay, ole girl. This is as good as it gets." She grabbed her purse off the seat, shut the squeaky car door, and headed across the parking lot to the office buildings. If the interview was with the younger Wade brother, she might have a fighting chance at getting the job. Her resume' wasn't great, with her work experience consisting of positions like grocery store checker, coffee barista, snow cone stand worker, and house cleaner. The letter from her college advisor with its awesome recommendation and praise for her skill with numbers would surely count for something, though. Wade Brothers Construction called her. Somebody obviously thought she was qualified to work there.

She pulled open the heavy glass door to the front of the building, and a waft of icy air swirled around her as she stepped into the room. She blinked a couple of times, waiting for her eyes to adjust from the bright sunlight to the soft glow of the business office. *Oh, man.* She started across the room to the desk sitting near a set of stairs and the tingling sensation of goosebumps struck the naked flesh of her calves. She would have prickly legs by the time she reached the top of the stairs for sure now. Goosebumps always made the hairs pop back out.

"Hello. I'm here for the two o'clock interview you contacted me about."

"Hello." The thin woman with the short, salt and pepper hair smiled up from the desk. "Go on up the stairs to the first door on your right. I will let Mr. Wade know you have arrived."

"Thank you." Fiona looked over her shoulders to the empty chairs in the reception area. Was she the only one they had contacted for the job? She kept her resume' updated at the job center and had stopped by the place first thing this morning to let them know she was once again looking for employment. The job center never actually helped her find a job. If she hadn't gotten the call today for this interview, she would have sworn that they never sent her resume' out to places looking to fill positions. Maybe things were looking up and the coffee shop fiasco yesterday was an answer to the little prayer she sent up yesterday morning. If she wanted to get a business degree, it would be great to experience working in a business setting while she saved to go back to school.

Fiona's knuckles rapped softly against the wooden door. She opened the door and stepped inside onto thick dark blue carpet, rather plush for an office setting. Her eyes roamed the room, taking in the dark paneling with the different paintings of ships on the ocean adorning the walls in their broad frames. Her eyes stopped at the enormous cherry wood desk in front of the floor to ceiling windows framed with dark blue curtains.

The furnishings in the room probably cost more than our entire little house. Fiona swallowed, but her tongue remained glued to the top of her mouth, dry as a bone.

"Take a seat, Miss Madison."

Fiona's head jerked to the right; the man's deep voice was

unmistakable. Langston Wade stepped through a doorway in the far corner of the room, wiping his hands on a paper towel. He grabbed one shirt sleeve and started rolling it down from his elbow. Fiona quickly pulled her eyes away from his muscular forearms and up to his face. "I, uh." She paused and raked her dry tongue over her equally dry lips. "I am here for the job interview."

"Yes, take a seat."

Langston Wade nodded toward the leather chair a few feet from where she was standing, and she made her way over to where it was. She gave a quick tug on her skirt and sat in the chair; Langston settled into a second leather chair behind the desk. She watched, her eyes transfixed, as he rolled his second sleeve down and buttoned his cuffs into place at the wrists. Why were his sleeves not the least bit wrinkled while her sweater seemed to wrinkle if she breathed too deep?

Langston Wade finally finished with his sleeves and leaned back in his chair, staring at her. "Are you interested in working for me?"

"Yes." The word came out in a high-pitched squeak. Fiona cleared her throat and spoke a second time. "Yes, I am."

"Good. It will be Monday through Friday, 8:00 to 5:00, with an hour off for lunch. I will get a list of your duties ready, and you can start next week."

"Can I do 8:30 to 5:00 with thirty minutes for lunch instead?" Fiona bit her lower lip as she looked across at the man's stern expression. One thing she had learned from her time at the coffee shop was that she needed hours where she could get to work on time without having to try to sneak in late. If she could get this settled before she started, it would prevent any problems with this job, and she desperately needed this job. "I have a prior obligation every morning that

I cannot get out of. It really won't take me an hour to eat lunch, anyway."

"That won't be a problem." Langston brought his fingertips together, forming a tent in front of his chin. "Do you have a reliable way to get to work? You can use my Tahoe for the errands you will have to run for the job, but I expect you to get to and from work in your own vehicle."

"Yes. I have a car." Fiona adjusted her hips in the chair, trying not to fidget under his serious gaze. He had to recognize her from yesterday, and all of his other trips into Bayou Bean. It appeared he was going to give her the job, anyway.

"Okay." Langston suddenly sat forward and rolled his chair closer to his desk. "You can start Monday morning at 8:30." He picked up a pen from the desk and scribbled something on a piece of paper. "Here's my address. You can wear jeans and a shirt or whatever, as long as it's something you can work in and won't . . . trip you up." He stretched his hand holding the paper across the desk. "I will be there on Monday to show you how to get in and turn off the alarm and introduce you to Lester."

"Your address?" Fiona's brow pulled low, and she took the paper from his outstretched hand. "I know how to get here."

"Here? Why would you come here? No. Come straight to my house."

Fiona looked down at paper then lifted her chin, slowly looking back at Langston Wade. "Aren't you hiring me to work here in your office?"

"Here in the office?" A look of confusion washed across his face. "No. Didn't Mrs. Dean tell you what you are going to be doing?"

"No. She didn't." Fiona coughed and tugged at the edge of her skirt, now a good two inches above her knees. "Who is Mrs. Dean?"

"My secretary. The woman downstairs. The woman who called you earlier."

Fiona stared across the desk; eyes stretched wide. "I think I'm missing something."

"Okay, let me start over." Langston sat back in the chair again. "I assumed my secretary had taken care of all of that. My housekeeper had to go out of town and will be away for an unknown amount of time. Mrs. Dean said that you do this kind of work for the mayor and would be great to fill in until my housekeeper returns."

"Oh." Fiona listened to Langston Wade explain about her new job. Heat climbed up her neck. Housekeeper, not office assistant. "I see."

"So, do you still want the job? It's just me in that big house, but I need someone to do the wash, keep the place clean, buy the groceries, things like that. I'm sure you can handle it if you can keep Mayor Landry happy."

"I can handle it." Fiona pulled in a deep breath and let it out slowly. It was not the job she necessarily wanted, but the bills would not stop coming in because she was not making a paycheck. "Yes, I want the job. I will see you on Monday."

Langston Wade stood, walked around the edge of the desk, and for the first time since Fiona had entered the room, his face softened from the hard business exterior he seemed to wear so easily. "I went by the coffee shop this morning to apologize for how I handled the mishap yesterday. Sarah told me you lost your job because of what happened. I am genuinely sorry about that." He paused and stuck his hand out to shake hers. "I hope this job will help tide you over until another one comes available."

Fiona stood. Langston walked around the desk in her direction. She looked at his face and her lips turned up into a slow smile. He stepped closer, and a ripple ran through Fiona's stomach. "Thank you, Mr. Wade," she whispered, looking down at his outstretched hand. "I appreciate you thinking of me." She raised her hand and placed it in his, feeling the warmth of his palm as it pressed against hers.

"Call me Langston," he said, giving her hand a gentle squeeze. "Until Monday then?"

"Yes." Fiona looked from his hand up to his face. "Monday."

CHAPTER SEVEN

*L*angston ran a comb through his short blond hair one more time and walked out of the bathroom. A pile of damp towels lay on the floor in the corner, and another pile of dirty clothes lay in a separate pile near the door. He did not make it by the cleaners on Friday afternoon and was wearing his last white dress shirt. An empty take out box from the Gumbo Hut set on his dresser. He picked it up and left his bedroom, careful to hold it away from his shirt in case some of the étouffée from last night's dinner was on the box.

He glanced at his watch and hurried down the staircase and to the kitchen. Fiona should arrive in ten minutes. The interview had not gone exactly like he had envisioned. Mrs. Dean had only smiled when he asked her why she did not warn him that the housekeeper for the mayor was the woman who spilled the coffee on him the day before.

He had been washing his hands after lunch and heard his office door open. It had taken a few seconds to get his surprise under control when Fiona entered the room, but luckily, she had not seen him stepping out of the bathroom until he had mastered his expression. Fiona Madison, in a form fitting skirt and sweater, was a sight to behold. How had he not noticed this woman at Bayou Bean? The loose-fitting skirts and tee-shirts she wore at the coffee shop were excellent camouflage for the lovely woman who had arrived for the interview.

He stepped over to the trash can and threw away the takeout box. A low chuckle escaped from his lips. What would the chameleon Fiona Madison show up looking like today?

The soft ding of the front door chime sounded. Langston wiped his hands on a nearby dish towel. He looked around at the sink full of dishes and unkept counters. *When did I get so messy? I wonder how much I'm paying her. It may not be enough.* The door chimes sounded again. Langston stepped over a mop left in the floor from last night, where he cleaned up a spill of the only jug of sweet tea in the house. Hopefully, Fiona would be able to make decent tea.

He opened the front door and stared at the woman standing there. An unexpected grin spread across Langston's face. A tie-died scarf held a mass of deep brown curls away from her face. A loose-fitting tee-shirt and faded blue-jean overalls hid the figure he had glimpsed yesterday. He looked down at the Converse with the strings securely tied, but still flopping on either side of the shoe. "You sure those shoe-strings aren't going to be a problem?"

"Hello to you too, Mr. Wade." Fiona looked down at her shoes. "No, everything is under control, I assure you."

"Okay then." Langston stepped to the side of the door-frame. "Let me show you your list of duties, and afterwards I will leave you to get to work."

Fiona followed Langston Wade from the foyer, through a living room that looked like it came out of Veranda magazine, and into a kitchen that looked like a bomb had exploded in the recent past.

"Everything is a mess from the weekend," Langston said, looking over his shoulder at the kitchen door. Before we go in there, let me show you the office for the house accounts.

Langston opened a door off the kitchen into a room with a desk and a chair facing a large picture window overlooking a lush green yard. "That's Lester's yard. Whatever you do, don't let him out of his yard. He wreaks havoc on the pool area. He gets on the patio furniture and pretty much destroys it."

"Lester?"

Langston picked up a small silver whistle from the corner of the desk and blew. She didn't hear a thing, but within seconds, the biggest dog Fiona had ever seen in her life stuck his head out from a red and white doghouse in the back corner of the yard. The dog stretched his enormous tan frame, shook from one end to the other and ambled toward the back of the house.

"He's as big as a pony, or small cow," Fiona said, watching the dog walk up to an empty food bowl near the window. He looked at the bowl, then up at the window, and let out a long, sad yawn.

"We'll feed him in a second. Lester is an English Mastiff. He's kind of slow and easy-going, but he gets cranky when his food is late." Langston reached over and tapped the keyboard in front of the computer monitor on the desk. "Here is a list of your weekly schedule. You need to go to the dry cleaners and buy groceries today. You'll take Lester to the groomers every Wednesday."

"Okay." Fiona stepped a little closer and looked at the list of chores. She leaned in toward the desk and a faint scent of a woodsy aftershave caught in her nose. "Do you have accounts at these places, or will I need to get a check or cash from you?"

"Here's the house debit card." Langston slid open a drawer on the desk. "That's house cash," he said, pointing to a thick envelope, "and there's a checkbook with a few signed checks. I seldom use checks though. Get receipts any time you use money from this account." He touched the keyboard again. "Adjust the ledger with the debits. You can use the Tahoe for running the errands. Keep it gassed up and run it through the car wash every week too. You can pay for you lunch out of this account if you are out and get hungry. Just put the card back at the end of every day."

Fiona looked at the accounting system on the computer screen and smiled. She would love this part of the job. Balancing accounts was second nature to her. A swell of something filled her chest. Langston Wade trusted her with his house accounts. "I will make sure everything balances. Don't worry." A howl drew her attention back to the window. "I think he's ready to eat."

Fiona followed Langston out to the backyard and watched him open the door of a small shed. He ripped open a one-hundred-pound sack of dry dog food. The dog stood nearby and examined Fiona with bored, droopy eyes. Langston stepped out of the shed and bent down, pouring an unbelievable amount of food into the animal's bowl. The dog came to life and licked Langston's cheek and neck with his slobbery pink tongue. Fiona reached over and rubbed the gentle giant behind his floppy ears. Hopefully, the dog would follow commands, or getting him into the vehicle to go to the groomers would be a real chore.

Langston filled Lester's water bowl from the spout nearby. "Now let me show you the house, then I have to get to work," he said, holding open the door for her to return inside the house. "You can text me or call me on my cell if you have any questions."

Fiona followed him up the short hallway back into the ransacked kitchen. Despite the messiness, it was still a very impressive room. The appliances were all stainless steel, and she had never actually seen a refrigerator that you walked into like a closet. "Do you have a grocery list, or can you tell me what you like to eat?" She watched him open a pantry door where he kept the canned goods and staples. She would buy groceries like she was told, but there was enough food there already to last one man for a couple of months.

"Yes, I have a list. Hold on a second."

Langston disappeared back into the kitchen, and Fiona looked at the shelves filled with cake mixes, cookie mixes, brownie mixes, and cheesecake mixes. Langston Wade had a sweet tooth.

Crash!

Fiona stepped into the kitchen. "What happened?" Her eyes stretched wide, and she hurried over to Langston laying on the ceramic tile floor, eyes tightly shut and a grimace on his face. "Do I need to call an ambulance?" She knelt down beside him, unsure what to do. She looked around his head and up and down his body. No blood, thank goodness.

"I tripped over that stupid mop." Langston opened his eyes and took a deep breath.

"Uh, what do I do? Are you hurt?"

"Just give me a minute. I twisted my ankle."

Langston stared at the ceiling, taking a few more slow, deep breaths. Fiona bit her lower lip, unsure of what to do. Finally, he lifted up on his elbows and sat up, his skin a pasty shade of white.

"Are you sure you're okay?" she asked. "Your face is the color of a fish belly."

"Yeah, just a little queasy. I've either sprained or broken my right ankle." He slid his hand from his pant pocket holding his cell phone and tapped the screen. He looked at it for a second, then laid the phone on the floor beside him. "Lucas isn't answering." He pulled in another deep breath, blew it out slowly, and looked at Fiona. "Do you think you can help me get to my truck? I need to go to the emergency room and have it x-rayed."

"Of course." Fiona frowned and looked at his foot and then back at his face. "You can't drive though, not with a broken ankle."

"I probably can once you help me get in the truck."

"Yeah, right." She scooted down to his feet. "Which ankle?" She gently pulled up his left pant leg, and he winced. "Okay, the left ankle," she said, glancing up at his pale face. "Uh, we need to get that shoe off."

"Pull it off. Just warn . . . oh geez, I said warn me!"

"You don't have to bark." Fiona laid the black dress shoe to the side. "Man, that's a lot of swelling." She looked at his face, even paler than before. "Sorry. I figured it was best to just get it over with. Okay. Reach up and grab the counter with your right hand."

Fiona squatted near Langston's shoulders and helped him drape his arm around her. "Now, push up with your good leg, and, uh, tell me if you think you might throw up."

Although they were not graceful, and Langston almost tripped over the mop again, they finally stood. He held onto the counter and the wall on one side and Fiona on the other and hopped through the kitchen and out to the garage.

"Okay. Help me get behind the wheel."

"I don't think so." Fiona raised an eyebrow and looked up at the man beside her. "You almost passed out when we finally got you up. There's no way I'm helping you get behind the wheel of that truck."

"Nobody has ever driven my truck but me."

"Boo hoo. It's a truck, not an aircraft carrier. I think I can get us to the hospital."

"I guess you are right. Stop by the office on the way and let Mrs. Dean know I'm going to be late."

"Uh huh." Fiona rolled her eyes. They hobbled around to the passenger's side, and she helped him get into the seat. She went back and climbed behind the wheel. She stared at the garage door, then looked over at Langston. His head lay back against the seat, a sheen of sweat on his brow.

"Push the brown button on the key chain," he said, not opening his eyes.

"Thanks."

"Don't forget your seatbelt."

Fiona pushed the button, and the garage door raised. She pushed a black button, and the truck engine started. She had never driven a vehicle this nice. She adjusted the seat and mirrors, then eased out onto the circle drive and down the hill to the road. "I'm not stopping by your office. I'll call your secretary once we get to the hospital."

"Turn signal."

"Hush up and ride. Your eyes aren't even open."

CHAPTER EIGHT

*L*angston sucked in a gulp of air and restrained the moan wanting to escape from his lips. The brawny male nurse assisted him, none too gently from his wheelchair, into the passenger's side of his truck. The past three hours of x-rays, poking, prodding, and explanations of how he hurt his ankle had wounded his pride. Plus, everyone and their grandma wanted to know what had *really* happened at Bayou Bean, especially since the cute gypsy looking barista had gotten fired.

"Make sure he ices that ankle and keeps it elevated for the next couple of days," the nurse said to Fiona, sitting across from Langston behind the steering wheel.

"I will. I have the instructions you printed off and will get the prescription the doctor called in."

Langston glared at Fiona's smiling face. She talked to the male nurse about him like he was an invalid. "If that's everything," he said, looking back at the nurse, "I am ready to leave."

"Don't forget to buckle up." The nurse grinned at

Langston as he winked at Fiona. He closed the truck door and lifted his hand, giving a quick wave.

"We need to stop by the drugstore and my office before going home." Langston scooted his hips back in the seat and winced. His left ankle, wrapped in an ace bandage, brushed against the side of the truck floorboard. "Could you call me in an order to the Gumbo Hut and run pick it up?"

"We are going through the drive through at the pharmacy, then straight home. The doctor said to keep that foot elevated and ice it. You can't do that while we are in the truck."

"I need to let Mrs. Dean know what's going on," Langston said. Fiona wheeled the truck out of the emergency room parking lot, and he leaned forward and grabbed the dashboard. "I won't be in there long."

"I've already called Mrs. Dean and told her what happened. She knows you aren't coming in today, or probably for a few days."

They slammed to a stop at the red light, and Langston glared at Fiona. She didn't even bother to look in his direction. "I need to talk to her myself about some things that have to be done today." Langston clenched his jaw, voice calm and even. "It will only take a minute."

"Use your cell phone."

"I need to speak to her face to face."

"Facetime her." Fiona glanced over at Langston and smiled. "The doctor said to take you home. I'm taking you home."

"Fiona." Langston said her name slowly, like he was talking to a two-year-old who was not understanding what the adult was trying to explain to her. "This is my truck, and I am your employer. Take me to my office. It's not a request."

"Nope." Fiona glanced over at Langston again, a twinkle in her eye. "Sorry. Doctor's orders trump your grumpy boss face. I'll fix us something to eat when we get to your house and give you one of the pain pills we are picking up. Then you won't be so grouchy."

"I'm not grouchy," Langston snapped, grabbing the dash again as Fiona turned sharply in to the pharmacy parking lot. "Where did you learn to drive, anyway? You're slamming me all over the place."

"Sorry about that. My little car handles better than this tank of a truck." They came up to the drive through section of the pharmacy, and Fiona rolled down the window. She gave Langston's name to the pharmacy tech and paid for his medicine with the house account debit card. They rode the rest of the way home in silence. Langston stared out the windshield, refusing to look at Fiona, much less speak to the hardheaded woman.

Fiona pulled the truck into the garage and looked at her patient. "See, you made it home in one piece."

Langston climbed out of the truck and hobbled into the house, leaning on Fiona and stumbling on the new crutches. "Move that blasted mop." Langston hobbled through the kitchen, Fiona on his heels like a hovering, overprotective mother. "Make sure you get all of this cleaned up before you get hurt yourself. The last thing I need today is to drag *you* back to the hospital. Although I think the nurse would be happy to see you."

"Do you have a bedroom downstairs?" Fiona asked, ignoring his comments. They slowly made their way into the living room, and she looked at the shiny wood railing on the staircase. "I don't think you should tackle going to the second floor for a few days."

"Yes, there's a guest bedroom down here," Langston mumbled. He limped over to a leather recliner near the fire-place and lowered himself into the recliner. "Did you say you were going to cook something to eat?"

"Don't you think you should go ahead and get into bed now? You have to elevate that foot, remember?"

"I remember." Langston jerked the lever on the side of the recliner, using more force than necessary. His feet popped up on the footrest and a low moan escaped his lips. "This is fine."

"Okay." Fiona held her hands up in front of her, warding off his bad attitude. "Let me fetch that ice for your ankle. After that, I'll fix you some lunch and get you a pain pill. Somebody is just a little grumpy."

Langston leaned his head back against the recliner and closed his eyes, not bothering to answer. He listened as Fiona's footsteps faded down the hallway toward the kitchen. What kind of woman had he unleashed into his home? Yesterday she seemed so mild-mannered, even timid. Today, since he hurt his ankle, she had turned into a drill sergeant. At least it was a temporary situation. Mrs. Butler would come back eventually, and his life would get back to normal. He listened as Fiona's voice drifted from the kitchen singing *You Are My Sunshine,* the tune a little off key. *Yeah right. More like, you are my nightmare.*

Fiona leaned over the skillet of bubbling sauce and breathed in the aroma of the onions and garlic. It took a little searching, but everything to make spaghetti was in his kitchen. She rummaged through the freezer and found a pack of frozen rolls. Feeding the beast should help his attitude. She slipped on a pair of oven mitts and lifted the pot of noodles from the stovetop. She poured the spaghetti through a strainer sitting in the sink as steam wafted up in front of her face.

The corners of her lips pushed up in a faint smile. Memories of cooking alongside her grandmother in their tiny little kitchen through the years flooded her mind. "That brother of yours can go from can to can't at the speed of lightning when he gets hungry," Nana said, stirring a pot of chicken and dumplings. "Most boys are that way. They don't get a lot better when they turn into men, but you keep their bellies full, Fi, and they lose their horns and turn back into the sweet fellas God intended for them to be."

Insecurity almost smothered her yesterday at the job interview. Wearing Callie's clothes and being in that high dollar office made her feel like a fish out of water. During the interview, it had taken all her nerve not to throw in the towel and retreat back to the job at the snow cone stand. Fiona could handle whatever came her way working at that little place. If she hadn't needed the money, she would have run out the door when she saw Langston standing in the corner watching her, no matter how much she wanted to work in an office.

Working at his house was different. Fiona looked down at her faded blue jean overalls, her comfortable clothes. Yeah, this uniform, this job, was all a piece of cake. She could do this with her eyes closed. Not just the cleaning, although the mayor's wife said she kept their house cleaner working one day a week than any other person had done working three days a week. Her other house cleaning client, Mrs. Ross, the wife of the Presbyterian pastor, always bragged about her.

Langston's sprain wasn't a problem either. Following the doctor's instructions was easy when her patient cooperated. Come to think of it, she was more at ease around him since his sprain than she was before the injury. She helped care for her grandmother, doing more and more as the Alzheimer's took over Nana's life. Langston Wade didn't need as much care as Nana, obviously, but he was definitely a lot grouchier patient. That was for sure.

Fiona dipped a pile of piping hot noodles onto a plate. Feeding the bear and getting him comfortable would improve his attitude. At least, that was the plan. Homemade spaghetti and a brownie for his sweet tooth would change him from a grizzly to a teddy. If not, she would follow the doctor's orders and ignore the man's surly attitude.

"Here you go." Fiona set the tray of steaming hot spaghetti and meat sauce and a sweaty glass of freshly brewed sweet tea across Langston's lap. "Here's your napkin. I have brownies in the oven for dessert." He picked up his fork, and she ignored the scowl on his face. "There's the pain pill. Don't take it until you get a little food in your stomach."

"Thank you." Langston waited while she straightened the tray. He raised his eyes, briefly looking her in the face. "I hope you fixed enough for you too," he said, looking back at the tray.

"I did. I will eat in just a second. I want to make sure you are settled first. Can I get you anything else?"

"No. this is . . ." Langston paused as the door chimed overhead.

"Are you expecting someone?"

"No. I should be at work, so nobody knows I'm home except who you've told. Maybe it's Lucas. I texted him and told him what's going on, but he hasn't texted me back yet."

"I'll see who it is. It may be the UPS man or something like that."

"Unless it's my brother or Mrs. Dean, send them away. I need to get some work done, but otherwise, I don't want to talk to anybody."

Fiona wiped the palms of her hands on the legs of her overalls and walked to the foyer. She pulled open the heavy wooden door, admiring the ornately carved glass in the center. *Oh, good grief.* Danika Hawthorn's perfectly made-up face stared back at her.

The looks of surprise, doubt, confusion, and finally, superiority scrolled across the woman's features in a matter of seconds. The hairs on the back of Fiona's neck stood up. Danika raised her shoulders straighter and looked down her nose, like a cobra trying to enter Langston's house, and Fiona the watchdog was the only thing keeping her out.

"Can I help you?" Fiona pasted on a smile, ignoring Danika's snobbish glare. She had the unfortunate problem of seeing her from time to time when she was cleaning the mayor's house. If anyone ever thought they were it on a stick, it was Danika Hawthorn.

"Yes, uh . . ." Danika tapped a long, perfectly manicured fingernail against her sculptured cheek. "I can't remember your name. I'm here to see Langston."

"He's not seeing anyone today."

"He'll see me, honey. I'm his girlfriend."

CHAPTER NINE

The pain pill wasn't working yet, but he wished it was. Fiona and Danika strolled into the living room and Langston stared, a bored look on his face. They were as opposite in every way as two females could possibly be. Danika led the way, wearing a toothy smile that somehow reminded Langston of a shark. Her usual form-fitting dress and heels showed off her five day a week workout figure. The cut of her outfits helped her achieve whatever she was wanting—if men happened to be involved. Danika walked toward Langston like a tiger on the prowl. Fiona trailed on her heels, glaring into the other woman's back.

"Langston, darling. I bumped into Jet at the hospital and he said you were in an accident." Danika dropped her designer handbag on the nearby sofa and leaned over, kissing him on the cheek. "Are you hurt? Is there anything I can do?"

"I slipped in the kitchen and sprain my ankle." Langston shook his head, disgusted. Explaining what happened to every Tom, Dick, and Harry asking this same question over the next several days was going to get old in a hurry. "It's no big deal, and I would appreciate it if you would not spread it around that I was hurt or in an accident. I will be back up and going tomorrow or the next day."

"Oh, I don't know Lang. A sprain may keep you down for a while. I should move in for a day or two and take care of you." Danika ran her fingers through a few strands of blond hair near her cheek and turned to look at Fiona. "Get me a glass of tea, honey. My throat is getting dry."

Langston looked past Danika sitting down on the nearby couch to Fiona standing a few feet away on the other side of the fireplace, her hands on her hips. Langston watched Fiona's expression and forced back the smile taking over his face. Fiona glared at Danika, her eyes spitting bullets.

"It seems you are in excellent hands," Fiona said, staring down her nose at Langston. "I'm going to get your groceries and pick up your dry cleaning. Call me if you need me to do anything else."

Fiona spun around on her heels and marched to the kitchen without another word. Langston watched her march away, completely ignoring Danika's demand. This time, the smile did escape his lips.

"That little mouse has an attitude problem." Danika turned from looking at Fiona's retreating back and sat back on the couch, crossing her long legs. "What is she doing here, anyway? Isn't she the one that doused you with the hot coffee?"

"She is." Langston looked at the empty tray sitting on his lap. Fiona could cook. The spaghetti was much better than what Mrs. Butler made him. He picked up his tea glass and drained it of the last few drops. The brownies she had mentioned earlier would have to wait until she got back. Too bad.

"And?" Danika tapped her fingernails across the arm of the couch, watching Langston drink his tea. "Why is she here?"

"Not that it's any of your concern, but she's my new housekeeper."

"Oh, honey, I can find you somebody that will do a much better job than her." Danika watched Langston push the tray back as far as he could on the arms of his recliner. "Here, let me get that for you." She picked up the tray of empty dishes and sat it on the hearth in front of the fireplace. "Langston, you need to get over our little tiff about the engagement. We are a couple, you and me. It's meant to be. We can date as long as you want to. I won't mention marriage again until I am sure you are ready."

"We are not a couple, Danika. It's over. It's been over. I don't know how to tell you any plainer." Langston shifted his hips in his chair to find a more comfortable position. He should have gotten Fiona to help him to the bed before she left. Now he was stuck in the chair until she returned, but he would not be stuck with Danika. Not for long, anyway. "It's time for you to go."

"Langston." Danika smiled down and shook her head. "Let me get you a fresh pillow and make you comfortable. I can run to my house and get an overnight bag and take care of you until you are up and about again."

"I mean it, Danika. Leave. I made up my mind the night I broke it off. We are through. There's nothing for you here." He met her gaze and held it. "I'm not backing down."

He should have broken it off with her a long time ago, but he took the easy way out and let her hang on. No more. "You don't want to make an enemy of me, so leave while we are still friends."

Danika stared a couple more seconds. "Okay, but don't get too attached to your mousy little housekeeper." She leaned over and snatched her bag off of the couch. "You will scare her away, or she will drag you down." She ran her fingers through the top of her hair again and looked around the room. "Be careful, Langston. Situations like this are how rumors get started, and I know how much you value your reputation."

"Leave." Langston stared at the woman. *There's no way I ever had any genuine feelings for her. No way.* "Don't worry about my reputation."

She turned and strode out of the room without a backward glance. Langston lay his head back on the recliner and closed his eyes. The pain pill must have started working. All he wanted to do was take a nap.

Why had he ever dated Danika Hawthorn in the first place? She was beautiful, but cold, untouchable. Was that it? Was he so shallow that he would date someone for their looks and completely ignore their character? No. Danika was smart, driven and strong, things he admired, but she used her strength to always gain the upper hand. No matter what situation she was in, Danika was going to come out of it on top. She was like a leopard, beautiful, but deadly.

He had been attracted to her strength, true, but that was before he saw how she used that strength to manipulate people. She had slipped her claws into him and he had gone with the flow. She played the same game of cat and mouse with him she played with every other person in her life. Not anymore, never again.

Were all strong women that way? No, Fiona was strong, definitely not the mouse Danika accused her of being. She wasn't cold or untouchable, either. A dreamy sleep crept into Langston's brain. Different pictures of a tall woman with a mass of deep brown curls and stormy gray eyes wandered through his mind. Definitely not a mouse.

Fiona slipped a third plastic bag over her arm and slammed the door of the Tahoe with her hip. She opened the door from the garage to the kitchen with the tips of her fingers and dumped her armload of groceries on the counter. She looked around the room and blew out a puff of air. The counters were clean, and the dishwasher loaded, but she still needed to mop. There was a spot on the floor that her Converse kept sticking to every time she walked near the refrigerator. She would check on Langston, then get to work on the house.

Poor Nana. The nurse from the memory care unit called while she was at the grocery store. Nana had another urinary tract infection, and they couldn't get her to drink. Fiona rolled her head on her shoulders and hurried back to the vehicle to get the dry cleaning and last couple of bags of groceries. She had bought a bag of lemons and sugar with her own money. Last time, homemade lemonade, sweet enough to set your teeth on edge, was the only thing that would entice Nana to take in enough fluids to keep her out of the hospital. Alzheimer's was such a vicious disease. Nana wouldn't drink because her mind forgot what the thirst stimulus was, then she would develop a UTI. The urinary tract infection then made her memory worse. This was the third infection this year, and with every successive one, the Nana Fiona knew slipped a little further away. She pushed down the helplessness that wanted to engulf her and hurried to the living room. Time to poke the bear.

The living room was empty. The lunch tray set on the hearth, an afghan on the floor nearby, but Langston was nowhere to be found. Danika's car was gone from the driveway. Had Langston left with her? Fine. Her day would be easier with him out of her hair. When he hired her, he hadn't expected her to take care of him, just his house . . . and his dog.

She picked up the tray and started back to the kitchen. For some reason, she needed a hug. She sat the tray on the counter by the sink and went to the back of the house that led to the dog yard. She opened the door and spotted the English mastiff, lounging in the corner of the yard under the shade of an oak tree growing on the far side of the fence.

"Lester. Come here, big fella. We need to get to know each other."

Lester lifted his head and looked at Fiona, trying to decide if she was worth the effort of crossing the yard. He laid his massive head back across his paws without any attempt to stand.

"Fine, then." Fiona trotted across the yard to the animal. "You are obviously Langston Wade's dog. You don't come to me. I have to come to you." She dropped to her knees beside the animal and leaned her face in close. She scratched him behind the ears, the tension in her shoulders easing away. Lester lifted his head and his floppy pink tongue slathered her cheeks with dog drool. "And you are such a great kisser," she laughed. A picture of Langston's face, his brown eyes, his jawline and lips flashed through her mind. She wrapped her arms around the dog's neck, forcing the idea back into the *don't go there* section of her brain.

"You are a good boy, yes you are." The dog put an enormous paw on her shoulder, and she tumbled forward, her laughter ringing out across the yard. Lester scooted over and put both paws on her chest. Her cell phone buzzed, and she sat back up, pulling it from her pocket as she shoved off the dog.

"Don't attack my dog."

"Where are you?" Fiona sat up straighter and looked to the backdoor, but it was shut like she had left it. Her eyes scanned the back of the house and spotted security cameras placed along the eaves so that every angle of the yard was visible. She stretched her eyes wide and stuck out her tongue, then turning away from the cameras, she stuck the cell phone back to her ear. "Do you have remote access to your security system? Did you go home with your girlfriend?"

"Yes, I mean no. I have remote access, but I'm in the guest bedroom downstairs. I need something to drink and another brownie."

"Yes boss, right on it boss, hopping to it, boss." Fiona grinned as the phone went dead. "Okay lover boy." She leaned back over and nuzzled Lester one more time, then stood up. "Your owner is calling, and he's my bread and butter, so I'd better hop to it." Her phone buzzed again, and a text appeared on the screen. *Don't forget to wash your hands.*

CHAPTER TEN

$\mathcal{L}$angston looked down at the tray Fiona set on his lap. "Where's the brownie?" The bowl of vanilla ice cream and glass of lemonade looked good, but. "I really had my heart set on another brownie."

"It's under the ice cream." Fiona smiled and nodded at the tray. "I warmed up the brownie in the microwave and then put the ice cream on top."

Langston looked down at the bowl and pushed his lips into a thin line. "I really just want a brownie."

"Trust me." Fiona picked up the spoon and dipped it into the bowl, getting ice cream and brownie. "You want this." She stuck the spoon in her mouth and rolled her eyes. "Nana used to make this for us all the time." She held the spoon out to Langston. "Be brave and try it. If you don't like it, I'll eat the rest."

Langston took the spoon from Fiona and dipped into a much smaller portion. The two flavors hit his tongue and his eyes stretched wide. "Not bad. Tell your Nana this is pretty good stuff."

"She hasn't been able to make it in a while, but we used to have it all the time." Fiona turned her face away, reaching down and straightening the pillow under Langston's foot.

Langston watched Fiona fidget with the pillow. His spoon paused in mid-air. "Is she ill? I'm assuming Nana is the name of your grandmother."

"Yes, she's my grandmother, but more like a mother, really." Fiona took a deep breath and looked back at Langston. "She raised me and my brother and sister after our mother took off. We were little and none of us really remember our actual mother."

"I see." Langston lay the spoon down on the tray, the brownie momentarily forgotten. "Do you still live with her? Your Nana?"

"We still live in her house, but we had to move Nana to the memory care unit in the nursing home last year." Fiona swallowed hard and shrugged her shoulders. "She got to where she was not safe to leave at home anymore while Callie was at school and Sidney and I were at work. Sidney flipped the electricity breaker to the stove every morning when we left so she wouldn't burn the house down. But last February we had a couple of warm days and she wandered off. Somebody called the police when she came into their yard and sat on their front porch."

Fiona turned her gaze to the spacious window behind the bed. The afternoon sun shone through the curtains. A soft pool of light floated around Langston's shoulders. "She was six blocks away in her old nightgown, and the weather was getting colder. She came down with pneumonia and ended up in the hospital. When it was time to release her, our pastor and her doctor helped us get her in the memory care unit . . . and . . . that's why she doesn't make brownies anymore."

"Fiona." Langston reached up and touched her chin, bringing her face back toward his. "I'm sorry. I will pray for you and your family."

Fiona turned cautious eyes back to his face. She chewed her lower lip, not speaking.

"I wish I could say something to help you," Langston continued, "but I've never been through anything like that before. It must be incredibly hard to deal with a sick parent while helping to raise your little sister."

Tears dampened Fiona's eyes and sadness crept over her features, like a wall was lowering and letting emotions escape onto her face. She was letting Langston see a pain she guarded from people. "Putting her in the home was hard, kind of like we were failing her or something, but watching her . . ."

"Here." Langston scooted his hip over and patted the bed beside him. "Sit down. I'm getting a crick in my neck from staring up at you."

Fiona swatted a tear from her cheek and eased down to the edge of the bed. "I'm sorry I'm unloading on you. It's unprofessional, especially when you are hurt yourself. The last thing you want is a bellyaching housekeeper."

"No, I want to hear about it. Besides." He smiled and looked down at his ankle propped up on the pillows. "I'm not really hurt, just slowed down for a while. Mrs. Butler, my other housekeeper, was more like an aunt. She knew all about me, and I knew all about her." He reached over and patted Fiona's hand. "I don't need another aunt, but we could be friends."

"Can I call you Uncle Lang?" Fiona asked, a smile turning up the corners of her mouth.

"Absolutely not," Langston laughed. He picked the spoon back up and scooped up some ice cream and brownie. He held it to her lips and waited for her to take the bite. "While you tell me about your Nana, let's finish this before it melts."

Fiona swallowed the mouthful of her favorite dessert and cleared her throat. "The hardest part is watching her." She rubbed her lips together, searching for the words to describe the way she felt. "She is fading away. It's like I'm going and visiting a body that vaguely resembles Nana, but Nana's not there. She's been drained away."

"So, she doesn't recognize you anymore?"

"No, not often. Every once in a while, she'll smile at me, but most of the time it's only a blank stare." She shook her head slowly and looked down at her hands. "And her face is so thin, and sad looking, nothing like the sweet woman who took care of me all my life." She lifted her eyes and looked at Langston, her brow wrinkled. "Can I ask you something?"

"Of course."

"Why do you think God is letting this happen to my Nana? She loved . . . or I guess loves God. She read her Bible every morning and was always praying. She loved our church, and, in my mind, she is what a Christian woman should be. Now she's in the memory care unit and can't even remember how to take a drink of water. Why doesn't God take her on to heaven? Why is He leaving her here like this?"

"Don't take this wrong," Langston said, reaching over and taking her hand, "but do you want her to die?"

"No." Fiona's eyes stretched wide. "No, not at all. That's not what I meant. I just want to understand why . . ." Her words trailed away, and her eyes turned back to the window behind Langston's bed. "It's like she's dying in pieces. Like the part that made her my Nana is dying faster than the rest of her." Fiona looked up at the ceiling, and another tear escaped from her eyes. "I don't know how to explain it."

"It's okay." Langston desperately wanted to wrap his arms

around Fiona and tell her he would make it all better for her, but he barely knew her. Plus, what could he do to help her? Even with all of his money and influence in the town, she was in a situation that nobody, himself included, could truly make better. "I didn't mean to sound harsh. Have you considered that possibly God could be leaving your grandmother here because you and your brother and sister need to let her go slowly?" He watched Fiona's face turn back to his, her eyes blinking through more tears.

"What do you mean?"

"I'm not sure. I don't presume to know what God is doing," he said, rubbing his hand along his jaw. "But I wonder how it would feel to you and your brother and sister if she would have been snatched away in a car wreck or a sudden heart attack. Do you think that would hurt less?"

Fiona stared at Langston. "I don't know," she mumbled. "This is so hard, but I believe I understand what you're saying. It would be hard having her jerked away from us, too. God could be giving us time to say goodbye."

"It's just an idea." He reached up and brushed a strand of hair out of her eyes. "Is there any hope of her getting better?"

"She has better moments, but they don't last long. Now, a better time is that she eats half of what's on her plate." Fiona looked down at the lemonade glass. "Homemade lemonade is her favorite drink. I'm taking some by there after I get off today. I have to get some fluids in her, or she will end up in the hospital again."

"Doesn't the nursing staff do that?" Langston's lips pushed into a narrow line. "I would think they should."

"They try. They take excellent care of her." Fiona sniffed. She pulled her hand from Langston's and wiped her eyes. "They say she eats and drinks better for me, though. So, I guess she still recognizes something about me. Even if I can't tell it."

Langston watched Fiona stand from the side of the bed and step down to his ankle, that was resting on the pillow. She was ready to close the subject, and he would not push her. The way she dressed in her flowing skirts and quirky tee-shirts and tennis shoes made it seem like she was laid back without a care in the world. Really, though, she was carrying a heavier load than he ever had. Caring for a sick grandmother, working to pay the bills, taking care of a sister in school. His eyes narrowed. How old was her sister? He would find out. He wasn't sure what he could do to help, but if there was something, he would do it.

"By the way." Fiona turned and looked back at Langston. "How did you get back here to the bedroom? Did your girlfriend help you? No offense, but she doesn't come across as the Florence Nightingale type."

"First of all." Langston shook his head. "Danika is not my girlfriend."

"She *said* she's your girlfriend," Fiona said, dragging out the word. A mischievous twinkle danced in her eyes. "Maybe you don't know you're her boyfriend."

"Believe me. I know exactly who and what I am, and I am not Danika Hawthorn's boyfriend. Besides, she left right after you did."

"If you say so," Fiona said in a singsong voice, a tease playing on her lips. "So, if she didn't help you, how did you get back here?"

"I used my crutches and got back here by myself. I told you, this is no big deal."

Fiona poked her lips out. "The doctor said to stay off of that ankle for a few days. You heard him, Mr. Hardhead. You popped that pain pill in your mouth before I left. What if you would have gotten woozy and fallen?"

"I didn't," Langston said, irritation in his voice. "I'm not a two-year-old."

"I know, but you do seem to have a hard time following instructions. Kind of like a two-year-old," she said, mumbling the last few words under her breath.

"What did you say?"

"Oh, nothing."

CHAPTER ELEVEN

*F*iona unlocked Langston's front door and let herself into his house. "Lucy, I'm home," she called, walking into the living room. This was the second week of work after the fall, and they had developed a comfortable routine. At first, he insisted he didn't need the crutches, and could go back to driving and working as he pleased. After hobbling around without his crutches the morning after the fall, his ankle was swollen larger than day one. It was obvious he was hurting worse, but he would not admit it. He had taken a pain pill that afternoon and returned to bed before she left that evening. The next day, he agreed to use his crutches without any further problems.

After a long battle of wills, she convinced him to stay home from work the rest of last week. He did have some strings attached. She made a trip to the office at least once a day to pick up documents to sign or mail he needed to attend to or other things. Finally, she talked him into setting up Zoom with his secretary. It impressed him when she set up Mrs. Dean's computer so they were able to talk back and forth face to face like he wanted.

This week, he insisted on going in and working at least part of the day. "After all, it's my foot that's hurt, not my head," he said, Monday morning when she arrived. "I can still work. You can drive me there, do the errands on the list, then come get me a few hours later."

"The doctor said it's a bad sprain. You are supposed to prop that foot up."

"I can prop it up at work." He stuck his lower lip out and blinked up at her from the recliner. "Please, Mom," he teased, "I promise to be a good boy if you will let me go."

Fiona gave in, not that it mattered. Langston was going to do as he pleased anyway, but she was touched that he wanted her approval.

All week long, they ate breakfast together, then she drove him to the office at 9:00 and picked him up by noon. In the afternoons, she would finish the cleaning, then do whatever tasks he added to the list. He usually followed her around like a lost puppy, or either sat in the recliner calling her every three minutes, wanting to talk. She mentioned to Mrs. Dean that Langston was such a chatterbox. The secretary acted like she didn't know what Fiona was talking about.

"Both of the Wade brothers are rather reserved," Mrs. Dean said, raising her eyebrows. "Mr. Langston discusses business, of course, but I have to say I've never heard anyone call him a chatterbox. It's probably the pain medication he's taking for his foot that's loosened his tongue."

Fiona did not argue with the woman, but Langston quit taking the pain medicine on the second day of his injury. That wasn't it. No. The man loved to talk. That was all there was to it.

Fiona walked through the living room toward the kitchen and breathed in the unmistakable aroma of frying bacon. "I'm the one who's supposed to be cooking for you, remember?" She walked up to the industrial sized stove and looked at the six pieces of bacon on one side of the griddle. A pile of scrambled eggs big enough to feed an army took up the other side. "Whose coming over? There's enough food there for at least two more people."

"It's only me and you." Langston pushed the spatula back and forth through the eggs so they would cook evenly. "I figured I could go ahead and get breakfast ready, then we can get on the road a little earlier."

"Ah, I should have known there was a reason for you to grace me with your culinary skills." She stepped over and pulled two plates from the cabinet. "Where's your crutches?" she asked, looking around the stove. "I'm not going to drive you to your office if you aren't going to follow the doctor's orders."

"Slow down, boss woman." Langston nodded toward the kitchen table sitting nearby. "I hopped over here holding onto the counter. I put no pressure on my ankle at all."

"Well." Fiona's brow wrinkled, but her lips turned up at the corners. "Don't let it happen again." She set the plates near the stove and walked over and retrieved the crutches. "Now go sit down and let me finish this up. You get too handy around here, and I will be out of a job."

A few minutes later, they sat at the table with plates piled high. "I'll never be able to eat all of this." Fiona picked up a slice of the slightly burned bacon and nibbled the corner. "How many eggs did you scramble?"

"Six. We need our protein." Langston scooped up a forkful of eggs. "I was thinking last night. I'm sick and tired of being cooped up inside all day. When you come get me this afternoon, let's go for a picnic."

"Um," Fiona raised a skeptical eyebrow. "Are you sure you can maneuver your crutches through the park?" She picked up her coffee and blew the steam off the top of the cup. "Why don't I fix lunch on the patio? We can eat outside and get into the pool afterwards. You can remove the ace wrap from your ankle and swim off some of that nervous energy."

"Alright, I'll settle for that on one condition." He pointed a piece of bacon in her direction like a baton. "We go out to dinner this evening."

"Langston, you know I have to go feed Nana when I leave here. Besides, going to the office, swimming this afternoon, going out tonight . . . that's a bit much, don't you think?"

"I can ride with you to the memory care unit. I want to meet your Nana, anyway. Then we can run get a bite to eat somewhere. I just need to get out for a while. Nix the pool idea if we need to. I want to get out of the house."

"Well, I guess I could do that." Fiona looked across the table at the dimple in Langston's left cheek. It popped up when he smiled, reminding her of an extremely tall, overly handsome schoolboy. "Where do you want to go?"

"Let's go somewhere nice. I want to see you in a dress, and not one of them long skirts you live in. Something dressier, that doesn't make you look like you're going to grab a tambourine and start singing folk music."

"What's wrong with my skirts?" Fiona frowned. "I like my skirts."

"And you look nice in your skirts, but let's get a little dressed up, make it a special night."

"I don't know." Fiona lifted her coffee cup to her lips and looked away. "I think I'll have to pass."

"Awe, come on. Humor me just this once. Don't you want to eat someone else's cooking for a change?"

"I'm eating your eggs right now."

Langston reached across the table and took Fiona's hand in his. "Please go. For me."

The touch of Langston's hand combined with the expression in his mocha colored eyes made Fiona's breath catch in her throat. "I don't own a nice dress," she finally whispered. "Those old skirts are the best I have."

"Oh." Langston's brow drew down for a brief second. The solution popped into his head and his smile returned. "That's no problem. I'll get you a dress. What size are you?"

"How are you going to *get me* a dress?" Fiona looked across the table, her curiosity now peaked.

"Don't worry about it. If I get you something to wear, will you go?"

"I guess so." Fiona bit her lower lip. "I wear a size four."

"And shoes. You can *not* wear those Converse. What size? Six?"

"Eight."

He had it bad. He knew it. There was no denying it. Somewhere since the time Fiona had poured coffee down his shirt and now, he had fallen for her. Last night he had flopped around half the night, unable to go to sleep. The realization fell on him like a ton of bricks.

Every morning. the first thing that popped into his head was what ridiculous outfit she would show up in that day. He spent the day trying to make her smile, and at night he went to sleep, replaying everything they had done together. If one of his friends was acting like such a lovesick hound, he would tell him to grow up and act like a man. Since Fiona had literally stumbled into his life, he couldn't seem to get control of his emotions.

It was illogical, at best, to even consider getting romantically involved with Fiona Madison. Yesterday at his office, instead of working, he made a few calls and did a little research. On Google maps, a picture of a house in the poorest section of Carson's Bayou correlated with her address, but the place was an absolute dump. Junk, like car engines and a rusty swing set without a swing, littered the yard. The paint was peeling away from the walls of the house. Some windows were cracked, and the porch sagged so much on one end that he was sure all the wood on the tiny old home was rotten.

Fiona graduated valedictorian of her high school class. The information online from an old newspaper clipping said she got a full scholarship to college. She had excelled in math, with an extremely high ACT score. He could definitely see that this was true. She was smart as a whip. She had brought him a printout of his house accounts for the past year and showed him several changes he could make to save a little money, along with quite a few bookkeeping errors Mrs. Butler had made along the way. Going over those records animated her with an excitement he had not seen before.

The reason she dropped out of college was a mystery. It shouldn't have been financial. She had scholarships. Of course, she had mentioned that her family needed her to work, but would her grandmother have allowed Fiona to throw away her future to work at a minimum wage job? Maybe the Alzheimer's was already affecting Nana's thinking even then. It might have had something to do with her little sister. Callie was a senior, but back then, she should have been in her freshman year. Kids that age needed someone around to keep them on the right track. Working and going to college would have kept Fiona pretty busy. It fit that she would put her life on hold to take care of her sister, make sure she stayed out of trouble like a mother would do.

There had to be a reason she dropped out. Even for the short time he had known Fiona, a few things were obvious. She was definitely not a quitter, and she was definitely not lazy. She completely devoted her life to her family. She spent every waking minute working to keep them going.

At first, after staring into the darkness until way past midnight, he had tried to tell himself he could ignore this ridiculous infatuation with his beautiful housekeeper. They were from two completely different worlds, and the last thing he wanted in his life was disorder. Fiona Madison seemed to sprinkle the stuff like fairy dust every time they were together.

He flopped around on his pillow half the night, arguing with himself. The more reasons he gave himself to keep Fiona at a distance, the more he wanted to get to know her better. Finally, he gave in. He liked Fiona, deeply liked her. A warmth started to grow where the uneasiness had been. She didn't necessarily seem attracted to him, but she didn't really seem put off by him either . . . at least not most of the time. Could he win her over?

What could he do to entice her to see him like he was starting to see her? There was an attraction there. Every time their hands touched, every time they bumped into each other, he got this warm tightness in his chest. It seemed to be growing like weeds in a turnip patch on his side. Would it grow in her too?

She was always doing things for other people. She drove to the memory care unit every day before and after work to feed her grandmother. At night when she got home, she helped her little sister fill out forms to apply for scholarships for college. She packed her brother's lunch for work every day. She worked at the mayor's house two weekends a month, and one of the preacher's houses the other two.

Then there was all the extra work he had put on her because of his sprain. She waited on him tirelessly, always making sure she had his dinner cooked and waiting before she left that afternoon. She did all the regular chores on the list, plus cleaning up after him all day long and chauffeuring him around.

It was simple, really. He needed to do something for her. Something to show her he appreciated her. He dozed off to sleep with the plan to take her to the park for a picnic forming in his mind. He could get the deli to fix the food, and they could spend the afternoon together. She could just enjoy the day. When she mentioned the crutches, the flaws in his plan became obvious. She would have to tote the basket to the picnic table and set everything up, then clean up after they were done. She would be doing all the work . . . again.

She talked about the pool, but he was only halfway listening. A night out, an actual night out, would work better than the picnic. All she had to do was drive. Plus, using the excuse of needing to get out of the house wouldn't scare her away before he had a chance to let her see how he was feeling.

Now all he needed was to get a fancy dress.

CHAPTER TWELVE

Fiona pushed a wad of curls away from her forehead and stepped backwards out of the shower. It was bathroom cleaning day. It wasn't that hard of a task really, since Langston only used one. Nevertheless, it was time-consuming. There were five bathrooms in the house, and another one in the pool house. Nobody living alone needed six bathrooms, but that wasn't her business.

She looked down at her naked feet and damp jeans rolled up to her knees. Last week, trying to clean his walk-in shower and garden tub in her skirt had turned into a comedy of errors. She finally pulled the skirt tail up between her legs and tucked it into the waist, like it was some kind of sumo wrestler's floral diaper. Langston, of course, came in while she was rinsing the shower stall. He laughed so hard his face turned scarlet. She probably shouldn't have sprayed him with the detachable shower head. It only soaked his clothes, got her wetter, and made more work for her when she had to mop up the soaked floor.

Today he was at the office, and she could work in peace.

It was a good thing he changed his mind about the picnic. Not having to deal with all of that left a little more time to make sure she straightened everything up for the weekend. She did not officially work for Langston on Saturday or Sunday. He was supposed to cook for himself or go out to eat or whatever on those two days. Now that he had the sprain, she needed to make sure he had food for the weekend. He could be kind of grumpy, but overall, he was a nice guy. It didn't seem right to let him starve on her days off.

Fiona would only be able to confine Langston to the house a little while longer. He would insist on driving any day now, using his uninjured foot to push the pedals. It wouldn't hurt anything. He would then be gone every day, working at the office again. Her job should get a lot easier when that happened . . . but . . . a sad smile formed on her lips. She straightened the fresh hand towel on the hanger by the sink and turned out the bathroom light. She would miss their time together.

The door chimes sounded, and she walked through the house to the front door, pulling off the yellow rubber gloves. The lawn man arrived while she was driving Langston to work. He was probably finished mowing and needed her to pay him. She opened the door, but it was not the lawn man. A beautiful woman with long black hair, dressed in an expensive-looking skirt and jacket, looked back at Fiona, a pleasant smile on her face. How did this woman know Langston? Did every female in his life look like a Barbie or a model? Geesh.

"Can I help you?" Fiona asked, glancing down at her bare feet, wet jeans, and tee-shirt. Her faded green tee with the words *Spinach Is Good,* and holey jeans suddenly felt inadequate, even for scrubbing sinks and toilets and answering the door.

"You must be Fiona," the woman said warmly. "I'm Vivian Wade, Langston's sister-in-law. I have a few things for you in my car. Can I bring them in?"

"Um, sure." Fiona's eyebrows raised, looking past the woman to a little red sports car parked in the drive. "Can I help you with anything?"

"No, I can manage."

The woman went back to the car and Fiona hurried to the little office at the back of the house where she had left her shoes. She slipped on the dollar store flip flops, then stepped into the bathroom across the hallway near the laundry room. She looked in the mirror and pulled the yellow gloves from her back pocket, tossing them on the vanity. Curls were escaping from her ponytail in their usual crazy fashion. Her shirt was splashed with water. She smelled faintly of toilet bowl cleaner. Oh well, she was the housekeeper.

Fiona hurried back to the front of the house. Four boxes, such a pale shade of pink they were almost white, sat inside the front door.

Vivian walked up with three shoe boxes in her arms. "I could have gotten Dolly to deliver these, but I'm dying to see them on you, so I decided to deliver them myself."

"This is all for me?" Fiona looked down at the boxes and then back at the black-haired woman. "I guess Langston had you do this. I hope you didn't go to a lot of trouble."

"It's no trouble." Vivian stepped into the foyer and pushed the front door shut with her backside. She smiled at Fiona. "I love shopping, and I'm dying to see which dress you pick for tonight." Vivian glanced at the living room and then at the staircase. "Why don't we go upstairs to one of the extra bedrooms to look at everything?" She shoved the shoe boxes into Fiona's hands and reached down to retrieve the other packages. "You are going to knock Lang's socks off tonight."

Fiona walked behind Vivian up the staircase to a bedroom near the front of the house, listening to Vivian chatter.

"Langston called and asked me to help him pick out an outfit for you tonight," Vivian said over her shoulder. They walked into one of the guest bedrooms and Vivian looked around, then placed her boxes on the bed.

When Langston said he would get her a suitable dress and shoes, Fiona figured that meant he would send Mrs. Dean across town to Target for the outfit. The boxes they carried up the stairs definitely weren't from Target. Almost everything she owned either came from the dollar store, a thrift store, or Good Will. These were boutique boxes from places she had only heard about.

Vivian spread the boxes on the queen-size bed for her inspection, and an uncharacteristic giggle escaped Fiona's lips. "Where do we start?" Fiona asked, staring from one box to the next. "Did this really come from Dolly's?"

"Yes, and she said if none of this will do, give her a call. As long as we let her know what we need before two this afternoon, she can get someone to run more options over here for us." Vivian looked down at the boxes and touched a finger to her cheek, like what she said was no big deal.

Dolly Babcock's boutique was as high end as you would find in Carson's Bayou. Their window displays, especially during Mardi Gras and Prom season when they had their gowns on display, were things of beauty. "I doubt that will be necessary," Fiona mumbled, her mouth gaping open. "I'm sure what you brought will be fine."

Vivian lifted the lid of the first box and pulled back delicate tissue paper. "Let's start with this one." She pulled a dress of flowing baby blue material from the box and laid it on the bed. "This halter dress ties behind your neck," she said, looking back at Vivian. "You could wear your hair up and it would show off your pretty shoulders."

Fiona's fingers raised to her lips, and she stared at the dress. The silky material gathered at the waist. Three tiers of asymmetrical ruffles flowed softly down the skirt. "I love the length. I'm not a big fan of miniskirts. My legs are so blooming long. I'm always tugging the hems down, trying to cover them up."

"So, you think this one is alright?"

Alright. If this woman knew what was in her closet. "Oh yes, definitely."

"Good. Let's look at the other one before you try anything on." Vivian slid another box over. "I love this one too. I'm glad you are the one deciding which one you will wear tonight. I think both are going to fit perfectly." She lifted the second dress and laid it on the bed by the first. Misty pink lace covered satin in the same soft shade. The dress, sleeveless with a boat neck and formfitting bodice, flared at the waist, falling into soft folds of fabric at the skirt.

Fiona examined the dress, words refusing to form on her lips. This dress looked long enough to hit her lower calves. She swallowed, pushing back the knot rising in her throat. "Did he tell you I like longer skirts?"

"He said you seemed to be more comfortable in them. He wants you to feel relaxed and enjoy the evening." Vivian leaned over and squeezed Fiona's shoulder. "I'm sure you already know this, but he likes you a lot."

Fiona's eyes stretched wide. She looked from the dresses to Vivian. "Uh . . . he's a good boss."

Vivian's eyes narrowed, then her lips stretched into a knowing smile. "Well, why don't you start trying on dresses?" She opened the next box and pulled out two slips, four pairs of lacy panties, and four identical lacy bras, all in different sizes.

Fiona looked at the underwear, a red flush creeping up her neck. "He didn't tell you to buy . . ."

"No, no, no." Vivian raised her eyebrows. "This was my idea, I promise. I figured since you were getting all dolled up, we might as well do it right." She paused, a slight frown overtaking her features. "Did I overstep? I'm sorry. I just kind of bought everything the way I would want to have it."

"No." Fiona let out a rush of air. "I was just afraid that you . . . or Langston . . ." she looked down at the beautiful undergarments, the words catching in her throat. "Had the wrong idea about tonight."

"Oh, honey." Vivian placed an arm around Fiona's shoulders. "Langston would never dream of taking advantage of you like that. He's not that type of guy." She leaned forward and looked into Fiona's down-turned face. "He's a gruff old bear sometimes, but he is a good man, a Godly man. This." She waved her hand at the underwear. "Was strictly all my idea. I promise."

"I think I'll try on the pink dress first." Fiona looked back at Vivian, her face cooling down. "I love the lace."

"Good choice."

Five minutes later, Fiona stepped out of the adjoining bathroom and twirled in front of the full-length mirror in the corner of the room. "Look how it twirls." She turned from side to side, admiring the folds of the skirt. "What do you think?"

"It fits perfectly. Here." Vivian opened one of the shoe boxes, then another. "You have the kitten heel or the three-inch ones. You're tall, but even in the three-inch heels, you won't be taller than Langston."

"I'd better go with the shorter ones." Fiona took the nude colored sandal from Vivian's hand and slipped it on. "I'll break my neck in the other ones."

Fiona tried on the blue dress next. It was as lovely as the pink one, but her love of lace won out in the end. Finally, Vivian opened the last box. A shawl, woven so delicately that it resembled a silver web, nestled in the tissue, along with a white clutch covered in seed pearls.

"You are going to look like a princess." Vivian draped the shawl around Fiona's shoulders. "Remember to snap a couple of pictures with your phone. What time are y'all leaving?"

"Time. Oh, snap." Fiona groped her leg, looking for her phone, but it was in the bathroom in her jeans. "What time is it? I'm supposed to pick up Langston at twelve thirty." She hurried to the bathroom to change out of the dress. "I'm surprised he hasn't called already."

"Oh, I forgot to tell you." Vivian's voice floated through the bathroom door. "Lucas is bringing him home. He said he would be here this afternoon. I think he's giving you time to get ready. I'm supposed to run his black Armani suit by the office. He said you would know which one he wanted to wear."

Fiona stepped out of the bathroom, jeans and tee-shirt back on, hair stringing around her cheeks. "I guess he thought of everything." She reached up and scraped her hair away from her face and returned it to the ponytail she wore on the days she scrubbed the showers. "Let me grab that suit for you."

Fiona waved to the little red sports car as it drove away. She would finish up the chores, about another hour's worth of work, then run to her house and grab a shower. She would do her hair and make-up there, but there was no way she was bringing that beautiful dress to her house. What if she snagged it on that nail sticking out of the bathroom door-frame that Sidney kept promising to fix? Nope. She would come back here and get dressed.

She closed the front door and sagged her shoulders against it. Langston Wade really was a nice guy. He could be her friend as well as her boss. There was nothing wrong with that. She pictured how he would smile when he saw her in the dress tonight and a faint flutter caught in her stomach. A friend . . . nothing wrong with that at all.

CHAPTER THIRTEEN

"Close your mouth. A mosquito is going to fly in and bite your tongue." Fiona descended the staircase, laughing at the expression on Langston's face.

The pink satin under the matching lace of the new dress swayed with her every step. "You look." Langston reached up and adjusted the knot on his tie. Suddenly, it seemed a little snug. "You look amazing."

Fiona's face glowed. "I adore the dress. It wasn't necessary, but I have to admit, I feel kind of special wearing something so lovely."

She doesn't have a clue how beautiful she is. Langston took a step forward and winced. *Stupid ankle.* He grabbed the crutches leaning against the wall and hobbled over to the staircase. "You are happy with what we picked out? I made Vivian Facetime me the dresses she thought would work. If you don't like them, we can swing by that shop and get another one tomorrow, and then go out again tomorrow night." *I'm babbling. My word. What has this woman done to me?*

"You did wonderfully." Fiona stepped off the bottom step and glanced down at her lower calves and shoes. Her pink toenails peaked through the little peephole in the end of the sandal. "I'm sure I couldn't have picked anything I liked any more than this dress. I even took time to paint my nails. I feel so . . . girly."

"Are you ready to go?" Langston leaned on his crutch and fished his keys from his pocket. "We have reservations at eight. I figured that would give you plenty of time to feed your grandmother without rushing."

"You can wait in the truck while I go in. I will try to hurry."

"No, I want to meet Nana. Besides, I can't let you walk around in public looking like this." He tilted his head up and down from her head to her toes. "That male nurse the other day at the emergency room was ogling you in your overalls. I might have to smack him with this crutch if he sees you like this."

"Yeah, right. That guy won't be where we are going anyway." Fiona laughed. "Wait until you walk in the memory care unit this evening and watch. You better keep those crutches nearby to beat off all the CNA's and nurses." He snorted, and she raised an eyebrow. "Just wait, Mr. *Armani Suit*. You'll see."

"See?" Fiona's voice floated across the table of the dimly lit Italian restaurant. Soft violin music played somewhere in the background, along with the faint click of silverware and occasional laughter from nearby couples, lost in their own conversations. Fiona breathed in the yeasty aroma of the warm bread floating up from the basket sitting between them. She leaned forward in her chair and smiled. "I warned you."

"She was not a nurse; she was a patient." Langston's brown eyes sparkled. "I think she thought I was her son or something. She kept telling me she needed me to take her home. I'm glad that nurse distracted her with ice cream, or I don't think she would have let me leave."

"I hope she didn't wrinkle the sleeve of your suit too badly. Poor old lady. She had a death grip on your arm." The waiter stepped up to the table with their dishes, and Fiona sat back in her chair. She looked at the plate of tortellini he set in front of her, then over to the linguini in clam sauce in front of Langston. "This is so exciting. Don't laugh, but the only Italian food I've ever had was made by Chef Boyardee or Prego."

"Trust me. This is much better." Langston stretched his arm across the table and took Fiona's hand. A shock of warmth ran up his fingertips. His throat constricted as he looked into her grey-blue eyes. "Thank you for coming tonight. I know you are just being nice to me after my fall, but I appreciate you agreeing to come."

"No." Fiona's voice caught in her throat. "I'm glad you asked me. Really glad."

Langston bowed his head and said a prayer of thanks for their food. He lifted his eyes and looked at Fiona staring at him, biting her lower lip. "Everything okay?"

"Yes." Fiona slipped her hand slowly from his and spread her napkin in her lap. "I am kind of scared to close my eyes. I'm scared when I open them back up that I'm going to be in bed, and all of this is some kind of crazy dream."

"So, you are saying you dream about me?" Langston's eyes wrinkled at the corners with laughter. "I'll have to remember that. Am I wearing my Armani suit?"

"No." Fiona grinned and picked up her fork. "You are wearing a white shirt stained with coffee and yelling 'Hot! Hot! Hot!'"

Fiona punched the alarm code into the box by the door leading from the garage to the kitchen. The truck door slammed behind her and she turned, watching Langston come around the corner of the vehicle on his crutches. "I'll come back and get our to go boxes in a second," she said. "Let me run to the bathroom first."

"Go ahead. I'm going out back to check on Lester."

Fiona hurried to the bathroom at the back of the house near the laundry room. She listened as Langston opened the door leading to the dog yard. His deep voice called the English Mastiff's name, then he switched to a much higher pitch and began baby talking to the giant animal. His suit would have to go to the cleaners next week after the dog finished drooling all over him. That was certain.

Fiona quickly slipped the beautiful lacy dress off and hung it on the waiting hanger. She turned away from the dress and looked longingly at her reflection in the mirror. The heavenly softness of the silky slip and lacy undergarments clung to her skin. She should take them off, too. Such nice underthings were not meant to be worn under her Good Will skirt and tee-shirt. She glanced one more time at her reflection, smiled, and grabbed her old clothes from the vanity where she left them earlier. She quickly slipped them on, not looking in the mirror again.

Her fingers caressed the pink dress one more time, then switched off the bathroom light. She hurried to join Langston in the yard out back. "You are ruining that suit," she said, watching him lift the dusty bag of dog food and pour some into Lester's waiting bowl. The motion sensor lights kept the dog yard bright, drowning out the dark sky full of twinkling stars. "You are already covered in dog hair."

"It's just clothes." Langston set the enormous bag of dog food back in the little shed and turned around. "You changed." He frowned, dusting his hands together and hobbling around Lester, already wolfing down the dog food like he had not eaten in three weeks. "We will have to do the picture with you in your usual get up. That will be fine, but I wish we would have snapped one before you took off that dress."

"Picture?" Fiona raised an eyebrow, then turned and looked behind her. "Your crutches aren't doing you any good propped against the house. I believe we've had this conversation before."

"I don't really need them anymore." Langston slipped his cell phone out of his pocket and reached his arm around Fiona's shoulders. "I'm certain when I see the doctor on Monday, he'll say I can get rid of them and start walking again."

Langston stepped closer and Fiona sucked in a gulp of air, his muscular arm encircling her shoulders. The palm of his hand rested against her upper arm. A warm blush started in her gut, rushing up her neck and into her cheeks. His arm pressed against her back; the heat warming the side of her body resting under the fold of his arm. "I, uh." She swallowed and tried again. "I forgot we were supposed to take a picture for Vivian."

"That's okay. We can take one now and do another one the next time we go out."

Langston's breath caressed her ear with every word, and a tingling sensation ran down Fiona's neck. "Next time?" She turned and looked up toward his face, his lips hovering just above hers. "Is there going to be a . . . next time?" Langston's face tilt down even closer and her lips instinctively parted. Should she pull away? Probably, but what would one kiss . . .

Langston's lips, soft, warm, brushed lightly against hers. The tingling from a few seconds ago turned into a full-blown bolt of electricity. Fiona's lips pushed up to meet his on their own accord, the words in her head suddenly silent.

Cool air replaced the warmness of Langston's lips and his touch much too soon. Fiona leaned in toward Langston, but he continued to pull away. Why was he stopping the kiss? She opened her eyes and grasped for Langston, but it was no good. He staggered backwards, slipping from her hands. Lester, obviously feeling a little left out, shoved his head, shoulders, and finally his entire body between the couple, determined to be in the embrace.

"Whoa, Lester." Langston grabbed the giant dog's collar to steady himself and stop the backwards motion, but it didn't work. Langston fell, landing hard on his backside, dragging Lester over on top of him.

"Aww." Fiona raised her hands to her mouth, attempting to hide her laughter. "He's giving you sugar, too."

Lester sprawled across Langston's chest, now lying flat in the grass. The dog licked Langston's face and neck, delighted to be part of this game. "Lester, enough already." Langston reached up and shoved against the gigantic dog, forcing him over on the grass beside him. "Are you going to stand there and laugh?" Langston asked, wiping the dog spit from his face with the back of his hand, "or are you going to help me up?"

"I'm not sure yet." Fiona grinned down at the man laying on the ground in the four-thousand-dollar suit covered in dog saliva. "It's kind of fun watching you."

"Give me your hand," he said, pushing up on one elbow, reaching his other arm into the air. "Aren't you the one that's so worried about me reinjuring my ankle?"

"Alright, but . . ." Fiona reached out and grabbed Langston's arm, but instead of pulling him up, she catapulted forward onto the ground beside him. "Hey, no fair."

"You shouldn't have changed out of the girly dress so quickly." Langston's eyes twinkled with a roguish glare. "I wouldn't have dared pulled you to the ground dressed like that."

"Ugh, Lester." Fiona raised her arm across her mouth, fending off Lester towering over her, determined to kiss her like he had done his master a few seconds before.

"Come on, boy." Langston pushed up off of the ground with his good leg and stood with very little effort. "Give the nice lady one more kiss, then we'll help her up."

"You are a devious man, Langston Wade," Fiona said, staring up from the grass. Lester backed away from her and sat obediently at Langston's side.

"But kind of cute too, right?" Langston reached down and took Fiona's hand, lifting her to stand like she weighed little more than a child. "You know I'm kind of cute."

"You're kind of a mess is what you are." Fiona raised an eyebrow at his boyish smile and turned toward the house.

"But a cute mess, right? Admit it. You think I'm a cute mess."

CHAPTER FOURTEEN

Fiona climbed onto the top rail of the step stool, leaned against the door of the stainless-steel refrigerator, and ran her hand along the top. She wrinkled her nose at the grime clinging to her fingertips. Nobody could see the top of the fridge, but it still didn't need to be covered in dust and grease. Yuck. She climbed down and walked over to the kitchen sink, turning on the water to wash her hands. Sandra, the regular Monday through Friday help, made the beds, cooked the meals, and did the light cleaning. Luckily, Sandra didn't do heavy cleaning. Even luckier, the mayor's wife didn't think it was extravagant to have a cleaning lady come every other Saturday to clean up behind the maid.

Fiona walked over to the mop closet and pulled out a spray bottle of Clorox cleaner, an old rag, and a basin to fill with warm water. It wouldn't take long to wipe up the grimy refrigerator. Unlike the hours it took cleaning the baseboards in the formal living room. Inching along on her knees with a pan of soapy water, wiping the baseboards with one hand, then drying with the other, had made the morning drag along forever. It wasn't too bad, though. The job had given her time to let her mind wander over everything that had happened Friday afternoon and Friday night.

The two exquisite dresses Langston bought her, now hung at home in her dinky little closet. If it weren't for that, she could have believed that last night had been a ridiculously wonderful dream. The tortellini in her refrigerator with a sign, *eat this and you die,* taped to the top, also proved the date, as she now thought of it, had definitely been real.

She would eat the leftovers for dinner tonight after she got back from feeding Nana. It would have been awesome if she could have figured out a way to bring home some gelato from the Italian restaurant. It was now officially her favorite dessert, The Blizzard she had gotten from Dairy Queen when she went out of town to watch Callie play basketball last winter didn't hold a candle to the gelato.

Nana might eat gelato, even though she wasn't eating anything else. Fiona methodically sprayed the top of the refrigerator with one hand, followed by slow, circular swipes with the cloth. Nana ate two spoonfuls of vanilla ice cream last night, and nothing this morning. Her grandmother's lips had clamped together, refusing to open, no matter how much Fiona coaxed, begged, and pleaded with her. The nurses said that when Nana let them put anything in her mouth lately, she would hold the food in her cheek and eventually let it drain back out. How could Nana have forgotten how to swallow?

Was Langston right? Was God leaving Nana alive because they weren't ready to let her go? *Dear God, if you are doing that, letting Nana stay here for my sake, please God, call her home. It's so hard watching her waste away. I know she will be better off with you. I don't want to watch her suffer if she doesn't have to. Please God.*

Fiona climbed down from the step stool, satisfied with

how the top of the fridge now shined. Cleaning the inside of the refrigerator was next, which wasn't that bad, since she routinely cleaned it out every visit. After she finished that, she had to wipe down the furniture in the mayor's study, and she'd be done.

An hour later, Fiona stifled a yawn, and she pushed open the door to the mayor's study. There was no denying it. The mayor had been smoking in the study since her last visit. The stale scent of the smoke clung to every surface. She crossed the room and sat the pan of water on the floor. Wiping down the furniture and vacuuming the curtains didn't remove the tobacco odor completely, but it helped. Everybody knew the mayor secretly smoked cigars in this room. Why was his wife trying to pretend he didn't smoke? The poor woman wasn't fooling anybody by not letting her husband smoke in public. If he could smoke outside, this room wouldn't stink like an ashtray.

Fiona could never stop Langston from doing something he really wanted to do, that was certain. He was about as hardheaded as they came. She squeezed the excess water from the cloth and started wiping down the leather chair behind the mayor's desk. Why was she comparing Langston and herself to Mr. and Mrs. Landry anyway? It wasn't like their date was anything serious. She rolled her eyes and pulled the drying rag from the pocket in her apron. One little night out at a fancy restaurant, and she was daydreaming about trying to henpeck Langston Wade. The corners of her mouth turned up in a smile. Langston had a sweet side, that was certain, but no one would ever accuse him of being overly tactful. The man certainly didn't keep his opinions about things secret, and he had a lot of opinions.

Fiona made her way around the room with her pan, wiping and drying all the surfaces that were safe to clean with water, and polishing the others. A trickle of sweat ran down the back of her neck. At least the first part of the job was over. She pulled out the ridiculously heavy vacuum cleaner from the nearby closet and ran the attachment over the drapes. Finally, she stood in the middle of the room and twirled around, spraying a fog of Febreeze in every direction. The temptation to sing *the hills are alive with the sound of music* in her best Julie Andrews voice always came over her every time she did this last chore, but if somebody heard her, they would think she was off her rocker.

"I don't want people asking questions about where the dresses came from." Fiona pulled into the church parking lot the next morning and killed the engine of the worn out Volkswagen Beetle. "Everyone has finally quit picking at me about spilling coffee all over Langst . . . I mean my boss. No need to set the tongues a wagging again."

"But we would look so good, Fi." Callie pulled a tube of lip gloss from her dollar store knock off Louis Vuitton clutch and mopped it over her lips. "You in the pink and me in the blue." She sighed and flounced back against the worn seats of the old car. "Joey Hebert's eyes would pop right out of his head if I came into the Sunday school class in that dress."

"First of all." Fiona pulled the keys from the ignition and looked over at her little sister. "We are not going to church to show everybody how good we look—especially Joey Hebert. Second. How do you know how you look in *my* blue dress?"

"I tried it on yesterday." Callie smacked her lips together and dropped the lip gloss back into her purse. "The shoes don't fit, though." She grabbed the car handle and jerked it down. The worn handle pulled away from the door, coming off in her hand. She glanced over at her sister and popped the handle back into place. "Hey, how's Nana doing? Mrs. Graham always asks for an update before class so she can pray for her."

"Not good. They haven't gotten her out of bed since Friday night. She didn't even wake up yesterday or this morning while I was there, much less eat or drink anything." Fiona reached over and straightened the dress seam on Callie's shoulder. "We can go today after church and visit her together if you want."

"I can't, Fi." Callie looked down at her hands, rubbing the pad of her thumb across her fuchsia pink nails. "You know how much I love Nana." Her voice caught in her throat, and she turned her eyes to her sister. "It just hurts so bad to see her like that. I just— can't."

Fiona leaned over and wrapped her arm around Callie's shoulders. "Hey. It's okay. Nana knows how much you love her. She understands." She raked a strand of blonde hair out of her little sister's eyes. "Maybe next Sunday night we can put on those fancy dresses and drive to the city. We could go see a movie or something."

"Really?" Callie ran the tip of her ring finger under her eye where a tear had escaped. "That would be so cool."

"Sure. Why not? We will be ridiculously overdressed, but what the hey."

Fiona and Callie parted ways at the church doors. Callie hurried to the youth class and Fiona turned in the opposite direction toward the college and career class. She couldn't bring herself to advance to the next age level. Most of the people in that group were either married or had finished college and were pursuing the career of their choice. Her career of choice was not scrubbing toilets and feeding Lester. Nope. Staying in the college and career class was a form of denial about her future, but she was not ready to deal with that denial today.

"Fiona, dear." Mrs. Landry stepped up to Fiona as she neared her classroom door. "Can we have a word in private?"

"Yes, ma'am." Fiona's brow wrinkled at Mrs. Landry's unusually stern tone. The woman was usually a little more polite when she saw her out in public. She followed her down the hall into the prayer room. The subdued lighting of the empty room covered her worried expression. She mentally went over her list of duties for the mayor's house. She had done everything on the list, she was positive. What was this about?

"Fiona." Mrs. Landry sat in an overstuffed wingback chair. She waved her hand for Fiona to take another one. The fruit scent of her perfume floated around her like an orchard as she watched Fiona sit. "Is there something you need to tell me?"

"No, ma'am." Fiona's eyes narrowed. "What's going on? Did I break something? The vacuum was working fine when I put it back up yesterday."

Mrs. Landry sighed and stared at Fiona through narrowed eyes. "Two hundred dollars is missing from my husband's desk drawer. I will not press charges, but I want to give you the opportunity to return the money and make things right."

Fiona's eyes stretched wide. "I don't understand." Mrs. Landry's words soaked into her brain, leaving a bitter residue behind. "Are you saying I stole money from the mayor's study?" The muscles across Fiona's shoulders tensed. "I am not a thief. I don't know who misplaced your money, but I did not take it."

"No one else has entered that study, Fiona." Mrs. Landry's jaw tightened. "If you didn't take the money, what happened to it?"

"I'm sure I don't know." Fiona pushed down the boulder lodged in her throat that suddenly wanted to choke the words away. "Please." She pulled in a ragged breath and looked into Mrs. Landry's eyes, skin smooth from carefully placed injections of Botox. "I did not take your money."

"Well." Mrs. Landry huffed and looked across the room at the stain glass window, at the hands folded in prayer. "I'm going to have to let you go until I figure this out." She stood and smoothed her hand over her pale green linen skirt. "If you remember anything about what happened to the money, call me. You might find it somewhere and bring it back."

Mrs. Landry pulled open the door and left without another word. Fiona sniffed and rubbed her fingers under her eyes. Six months. Six months of working her fingers to the bone for that woman. Doing whatever she said needed doing without a complaint, just a yes, ma'am, no problem, ma'am. Sure, I can do that, ma'am. Now they were letting her go at the drop of a hat, probably because the henpecked mayor had taken the money from the drawer to buy cigars, and didn't want to tell his wife.

She stood and pulled a tissue from the box on the little table between the two chairs. Callie would have to get a ride home with a friend. There was no way she was going to Sunday school now. If Mrs. Landry hadn't spread around her little tale already, she would as soon as she had a free moment.

Oh, Nana. I need to talk to you so badly. She looked at the stained-glass window. *Lord, I don't know what to pray. You know I'm not a thief and I desperately need that job, but right now I'm so mad I could spit nails. Help me God. I am so tired. So tired of having to deal with all of this by myself.*

She looked again at the window through tear-filled eyes at the verse under the hands. "Casting all your care upon him; for He careth for you." *Lord, please help me.*

CHAPTER FIFTEEN

*L*angston ran his hand along his jawline and stared across the porch at his little brother. "I don't think she could do something like that, but Mrs. Landry says Fiona was the only one in there. She was the only one who could have taken the money. She swears it's the only explanation for how it's missing. I wish Fiona was at church this morning to defend herself."

Lucas pushed the toe of his boot against the porch floor. The porch swing swayed gently in the evening sunset. He watched his older brother sitting on the steps a few feet away. "Have you talked to her yet?"

"No." Langston stared across the street to the house his brother used to live in. "You really should tear Mom and Dad's old place down and put up a house that matches the rest of the neighborhood."

"I have a lot of great memories in that house," Lucas said, following his brother's gaze across to the ranch-style house, so different from the other homes built over one hundred years ago. "Besides, the Bergerons couldn't afford the rent if I put up a newer home. I enjoy having them for neighbors."

Langston adjusted his shoulders against the wooden post, pushing into his spine. "I drove by her house after church. She lives over past Duncan street, as you're going out of town. I was going to stop, but I didn't."

"Why not?"

"Her place is really . . . run down. It almost looks like it should be condemned."

"Brother." Lucas stared down at Langston. "Don't you think that's a little harsh? The woman can't help being poor."

"No. That's not what I mean." Langston shook his head. "I couldn't care less how poor she is. What I'm saying is, I know she works three jobs trying to keep her family together. Her grandmother is in a home, her little sister is in high school, and her big brother works at a body shop. She told me he's wanting to open his own garage, so she tries to pay most of their bills on her own." An enormous orange tabby cat hopped up from the knockout roses along the porch and strolled over to where Langston was sitting. His lips flattened into a narrow line. "What I'm saying is, she probably really needs the money. Maybe she—I don't know — borrowed the money and was planning on putting it back later." Langston leaned down and nudged the cat away from the boot protecting his sprained ankle. "Mrs. Landry said it was petty cash. She wouldn't have even known it was missing if she hadn't been in the drawer looking for something else."

"There's a lot of people around here who need money, but that doesn't make them thieves." Lucas watched the tabby turn and go back to Langston's foot, and a spark of amusement flashed in his eyes. The cat was determined to rub against the orthopedic boot and Langston hated cat hair getting on him more than anybody Lucas knew.

The cat inched closer to Langston and scratched his face and neck against the corner of the boot. "I know," Langston said, irritation making his voice harsh. "Truman, stop. Lucas, call your cat."

"Not my cat," Lucas chuckled. "He knows you don't like it. That's why he's doing it. Just ignore him and he'll quit."

"I'm a man, he's a cat." Langston pulled his boot away from the animal and shoved the old orange tabby in his brother's direction. "I will not engage in psychological warfare with the neighborhood stray."

"Suit yourself, but you'll have cat hair all over that boot." Lucas leaned back in the swing. "When do you get to quit wearing that thing, anyway? Seems like you are milking this injury a little. I've noticed you're staying home and spending a lot of time with your new maid since your fall."

"I go back to the bone doctor tomorrow. I'm sure he's going to say I can stop wearing it. I would have left the thing off a long time ago, but Fiona insists I need to keep it on." Langston pulled his knee up, moving the boot away from the cat one more time. "Shew, Truman. You're covering me in your infernal cat hair." The cat finally lost interest and hopped off the porch, disappearing back into the rose bushes. "I have to admit, I have enjoyed spending time with her." A faint smile softened Langston's face. "She is so different. When you look at her, you think she's— flighty, kind of like a hippie or something. But once you get to know her." He paused and looked over to where Lucas was staring at him. "She's not like any other woman—any other person I've ever met."

"Bro." Lucas stared; eyebrows raised. "You're in love. I didn't think it was possible."

"I am." Langston let out a defeated sigh. "It's stupid. She is definitely not the woman for me." He leaned down and picked a cat hair off the black orthopedic boot. "Especially now that the mayor's wife has accused her of stealing."

"Look." Lucas stood and walked over to the steps. "You need to talk to her."

"You're right. I need to get this cleared up. It's driving me crazy."

"Yeah." Lucas stretched out the word as he sat down beside his brother. "But we both know that being tactful is not your strong suit."

"Says who?" Langston's brow wrinkled. "I run a million-dollar business. I can talk to people as good as or better than you."

"You can talk business. Talking to a woman you're in love with takes a little more," Lucas paused, "skill than you normally exhibit."

"Okay, Mr. love guru." Langston rolled his eyes. "Give me some words of wisdom from your great wheelhouse of experience."

"Just don't go in all guns a blazing. That's all I'm saying." Lucas shrugged his shoulders. "Let her see how you feel, and that you're on her side, no matter what happened with that money."

"That's what I was planning on doing."

"Well, then." Lucas raised an eyebrow, skepticism plastered all over his face. "What could possibly go wrong?"

Callie flopped across the twin sized bed and watched Fiona scrape her mass of chestnut curls into a reckless ponytail. "I'm going to ask Sid for the money. He'll get it for me."

"No." Fiona turned from the ancient dingy mirror and glared down at her little sister. "Sidney is saving his money to start his business. If we keep dipping into his kitty, he will never get there."

"What else can we do then? I can't pick up any more hours at the snow cone stand. I have basketball practice and debate team meetings and stuff to do with the school paper every day next week." Callie rolled over on her back and blew out a huff of air. "Why does high school have to be so expensive anyway? I can't believe Mrs. Landry said that about you. I almost wish you *had* taken her ole money."

"Callie!" Fiona turned back toward the mirror and picked up a tube of Chapstick. Had she been that childish at seventeen? "Don't say things like that. People will think our family is a bunch of degenerates."

"I said almost," Callie whined. "Everybody who has a lick of sense knows you wouldn't steal a tick off a dog, much less take money from the mayor." She stood from the bed and stomped out of the room. "Geesh, Fiona."

Callie was right, why *was* high school so expensive? It was her own fault. If she hadn't indulged Callie, letting her enter every club, group, and sport that fluttered into her head, the loss of this job would not be such a big deal. Nana's words rang in Fiona's ears. "Honey, if everybody else took a sip from the toilet bowl, would you take a sip too? Pick two things you want to do at that school and join those, no more." Fiona sighed. Little sister had turned up the toilet bowl and gulped it down.

Callie started spinning out of control about the time Nana went into memory care. Fiona could have said no when her sister was signing up for every whim that came along, but she didn't have the heart. Losing the only true parent her sister ever had made the teen want to fill the void with busyness. It seemed better to fill the hole with school activities, instead of other things girls her age could get into.

Now they were strapped, paying dues, picture fees, uniform costs, supply fees, and trip fees every other day. Oh well, she had created the monster. Now she had to pay the price, literally. But how?

Callie's head leaned around the door frame. "You could ask that rich boyfriend of yours for the money. I imagine he would love to help out."

"Langston is not my boyfriend. He's my boss." Fiona turned from the mirror and started smoothing the wrinkles from her bedspread. "I wouldn't ask him for money. That's unethical."

"Hmph. I hear how you say his name." Callie stepped into the small room and peered at her sister's few clothes hanging on the rusty old rod. The door to the closet had been missing for as long as the girls could remember. Her fingers stroked the satiny material of the blue halter dress. "Bosses don't buy women beautiful dresses and take them to fancy restaurants, but boyfriends do."

"He was just being nice because I had so much extra work when he hurt his ankle. He's a boss—just like Gary was a boss."

"I have never heard you say Gary the way you say Langston. Kind of soft and stretchy."

"Would you just hush?" Fiona picked up her feather pillow and pounded it with her fist, using a little more force to fluff it up than necessary. "I will not ask Langston for money, and that's that."

"Me thinks you progressive much, sister."

"Protest too much, you nut, not progressive. Now leave me alone."

"Did you talk to that other lady you clean for and tell her you're not a thief? The Presbyterian preacher's wife?" Callie stepped over to the dresser and looked at herself in the mirror. "She's not going to fire you too, is she?"

"I went by there yesterday afternoon after church let out. Mrs. Ross is a wonderful lady, and husband is a good man."

Fiona tossed the pillow at the head of the bed and looked around the bedroom for her purse. "She said she knew I would never steal, and that Mrs. Landry will come to her senses. That still leaves two Saturdays a month. I need to work, though. If Mrs. Landry spreads her tale around town, I'll never get another cleaning job to take that spot."

"What about Langston Wade?" Callie leaned close to the mirror and rubbed her finger across her teeth. "You better talk to him this morning before he hears what folks are saying. If you lose that job, forget my school money. You won't be able to pay your part of the bills at all."

"Come on." Fiona snatched her purse from under the edge of the bed. "I have to drop you by the school and go by memory care to feed Nana before work."

"Have you told him?"

"No, but don't worry. Langston would never believe what Mrs. Landry is saying. He knows me better than that."

CHAPTER SIXTEEN

"I need to meet with you and your brother together one day this week," Trina said, pulling Fiona into her office as she was leaving the memory care unit. "Your little sister does not have to come. I told Sidney when he stopped by yesterday."

"Sid came by?" Fiona's eyes narrowed. "Is everything okay?"

"Sidney comes by at least three times a week." Trina's eyes softened, and she placed her hand on Fiona's shoulder. "He sits and talks to your grandmother. You have a very sweet brother."

"He does?" Fiona said, surprised that Sidney had kept his visits from her. "What do you need to talk to us about?"

"Mrs. Madison's living will."

Fiona pulled the Volkswagen into Langston's driveway and shut off the engine. The nurse at memory care said Nana was not swallowing anything. Her grandmother's skeletal face flashed through her mind, laying against her pillow, barely pushing air in and out of her lungs. *Cast your burdens on the Lord.* She tried casting yesterday, but all her problems were still right in front of her with even more piled on. Tears welled up in her eyes, and she lay her head back, staring at the roof of the old car. Brown spots stained the gray material above her head. Right after Sidney had given Fiona the Volkswagen a few years ago, Callie sprayed a shook-up Coke can everywhere, staining all the upholstery.

"I promise it was an accident, Fiona," Callie had whined. "Besides, this car is so old, you wouldn't notice it, anyway."

Was Fiona's soul stained with brown blotches of sin like her old car? A verse about filthy rags pushed into her mind. What was that verse? It didn't matter right now. Right now, she had to pull herself together and get to work. She wiped the back of her hand across her cheek, swatting away a tear. Make it through the day. That was the goal. The rest of her troubles would be there to deal with after she finished her work.

She grabbed her purse and hurried into the extravagant house fifteen minutes late. Langston was understanding about Nana, but she didn't want to take advantage of him. She hustled through the empty living room to the kitchen. An open pizza box with one slice of pepperoni and nasty black olives lay near the microwave. An empty take out box from the Gumbo Hut set near the refrigerator. Eight empty ramen noodle papers were scattered over by the sink. "Good grief, Langston." Fiona picked up a stainless-steel skillet with a film of scrambled eggs glued to the bottom. "How can you always look so neat but let your kitchen get so messy?"

She picked up several empty bowls from the counter. A blob of something sticky and red, probably three-day-old ketchup, stuck to her forearm. At least cleaning up this disaster would keep her mind distracted. She filled the sink with soapy water, then went out back to feed Lester.

Where was Langston? He would not still be in bed. She rolled her head around on her shoulders. She needed to stretch some of the tightness out of her neck. Mopping would help that. Lester lounged in the doorway of his doghouse on the other side of the yard, completely uninterested as Fiona took his food bowl into the shed. Maybe Langston fed him already. He certainly didn't act hungry.

She hurried back inside to the little office to check the to-do list, even though she knew it by heart. The house was still silent, and nothing looked out of order on the desk. She jumped as her phone vibrated in her pocket with a new text message. *Gone to the ortho doctor. I figured you were busy with your grandmother. See you when I get back.*

The 8:15 appointment had slipped her mind. She could have gotten here early to go with him. Ugh. At least she knew where he was. *Sorry for being late. I think a bomb exploded in your kitchen, but don't worry. I will have it cleaned by the time you get home.*

A thumbs up flashed on the screen, and she slipped her phone back into her pocket. She hurried to the kitchen and stuck her hands into the steamy dishwater. Money. How could she make up for the loss of income from the mayor's job? She looked over at the kitchen table. An empty Styrofoam cup lay on its side. Something pink and milky dripped onto the tabletop. Langston loved strawberry milkshakes. He must have gone by the snowball stand over the weekend to get one.

The snowball stand. There was an idea. Callie couldn't pick up any extra hours there, but she could. Rusty, the owner, was always looking for people to pick up Saturday shifts so he wouldn't have to cover them himself. She could work every other Saturday until something better came along. Would Rusty hire her after hearing about the thing with the mayor's wife? He'd better. She had helped him out in a pinch more times than he could count when he couldn't find somebody to work. Plus, if she hadn't tutored him through Algebra two back in the day, he wouldn't have graduated from high school.

Fiona pulled a bowl from the water and started scrubbing the ramen noodle residue from the sides with a vengeance. The snow cone stand wouldn't pay as much money as the mayor's wife paid, almost half the amount, but every little bit helped. She would make it through this. She just had to work a little harder, that was all.

An hour later, Fiona plopped into a kitchen chair and twisted open the lid of her Coke. The faint scent of lemon cleaner wafted through her nose from the freshly cleaned counters and floors. She looked around at the gleaming kitchen, and a satisfied smile played across her lips. It was not a Brainiac job, or the job she wanted to have at this stage of her life, but it felt good to accomplish something today. Things were falling apart in some other areas, but she completed this task.

The low rumble of a truck engine came from the garage. Fiona took a long swallow of the drink and stared at the door. Langston had surely heard about the accusation Mrs. Landry was making. If he hadn't heard about it at church yesterday, Danika Hawthorn probably speed dialed him as soon as she learned about it. The doorknob turned, and Fiona bit her lower lip. He would understand.

"Look at you." Fiona's eyes traveled up and down Langston as he stepped into the doorway. "No crutches and no boot." She smiled as he made a bow. "Congratulations."

"Thank you. Thank you very much." Langston stepped over to the refrigerator, pulled out a Gatorade, and sat in the chair across from Fiona. "You didn't know I could do Elvis impressions."

"You can't." Fiona lifted her Coke bottle to her lips to hide her smirk. "Did the doctor give you any restrictions?"

"Nope. I'm free as a bird. I'm going to change and head over to the office in a few minutes." Langston took a drink of Gatorade and set the bottle on the table. "Before you get busy with whatever you have lined up to do next, I think we need to talk about what happened this weekend."

"Yes." Fiona sucked in a deep breath of air. "We do."

"I want you to know that I understand completely why you would take it. You have a lot on you since your grandmother became sick."

"Wait. What . . ." Fiona's heart thudded in her chest, heat creeping up her neck. Langston continued to speak.

"I will talk to Mrs. Landry and repay the money. Don't worry about that." Langston paused and reached across the table, taking Fiona's hand. "You don't have to do that kind of thing, Fiona. I can help you." He turned his eyes from her hand to her face. "I want to help you. I don't care what people are saying about you."

"You." Fiona's eyes bulged, not believing the words coming from Langston's mouth. "You think *I* stole that money?" Fiona spat the words out, like they burned her tongue. "You believe her?"

"She said you were the only one in the mayor's office. Danika said . . ."

"Danika!" The name screeched from Fiona's mouth. "Well, if Danika said it, it has to be a fact."

"Fiona, calm down."

"Oh, no you didn't." Fiona's nostrils flared, and she rose

from the table, jerking her hand from his. "Do you know what I told my little sister this morning?" Her eyes darted around the kitchen, a bitter laugh escaping from her chest. "Don't worry about Mr. Langston Wade. My job with him is secure."

"It is, Fiona." Langston leaned back in the chair, forehead wrinkled. "That's what I'm trying to tell you, if you will quit acting all melodramatic and listen."

Fiona glared down at Langston, disbelief briefly tying her tongue. "Well. Let me just get my poor. Little. Thieving. Helpless. Self. Together." A dangerous smile eased across her face and she picked up her Coke. "Mr. Wade. I appreciate your humanitarian efforts to try to help those less fortunate than yourself—especially when doing so might put your spotless reputation at risk. You are such a kind, good man. The less fortunate of Carson's Bayou feel honored that you live among us." She leaned closer to where Langston sat looking up and dumped the rest of the Coke on his head. "But no, thank you."

"Woman!" Langston's head jerked up, the brown liquid running down his face onto his starched, white, button-up shirt. "What is your deal with pouring drinks on me? I'm just trying to help you. Are you trying to get fired here, too?"

"You can take your help and . . ." Fiona's eyes darted around the kitchen, "stick it in your blender." She reached over and grabbed her purse. "Since you're a little slow on the uptake here lately, I will spell it out for you." She slapped a loose tangle of curls away from her cheek. "You don't have to fire me. I quit."

"Quit?" Langston wiped the Coke out of his eyes. "If you will calm down for a second and listen to me, we can work this out."

"I will send someone by later with the dresses and shoes."

She slipped her purse on her shoulder. "I will have to wash the underwear though, so please, don't go jumping to any conclusions. I will get them back to you. I'm not *stealing* them."

"Aww, come on Fiona." Langston pushed up from the chair. "Don't get all carried away."

Fiona glared at Langston, grey eyes sparking. "You have disappointed me worse than anyone I have ever known, and believe me, that's saying something. Goodbye, Langston Wade."

Fiona turned and ran out of the kitchen, through the living room, and out the front door. She fumbled with her keys, trying to focus through the tears. She finally picked out the right one and shoved it in the ignition. Her chest pounded in her ears, drowning out her car engine. The hole in the muffler needed to be fixed. Sidney would do that for her. She could count on Sidney. She looked out the window toward the house, waiting to see if Langston would follow her. A tightness squeezed her heart as she stared at the empty front doorway. *That's what you get for letting your guard down, Fi.*

The car eased down the driveway. Fiona stepped on the clutch, pushing the stick shift into second gear. All the fight suddenly drained out of her, and she pulled the little car over at the bottom of the hill, out of sight of Langston's house. *I thought you knew me. I thought I knew you.* Sobs flooded her chest, and she leaned her head back and let them flow. What else could she do? Tears flowed freely for five minutes, but that was enough. Crying didn't get things done. Thinking got things done. Who believed her? Who knew she didn't do what Mrs. Landry was accusing her of?

Fiona pulled a napkin from the glove box and blew her nose. She turned her car toward town. She had to get those dresses out of her closet. After that, she needed to visit Mrs.

Ross. She needed ice cream. There wasn't any in the fridge, and she only had twenty dollars in her wallet to last until payday. She wouldn't need gas to go back to this job. A no name box of fudgesicles didn't cost much at the dollar store. That would do.

CHAPTER SEVENTEEN

*L*angston adjusted his tie for the fifth time in three minutes and looked across the desk at his brother. "I have never seen a woman act like that before. She actually poured a bottle of Coke on my head because I tried to pay back that money for her."

"Let me get this straight." Lucas sat back in the leather wingback chair and stretched his legs out in front of him. "You've known this woman what? Six weeks? In this time, she's poured coffee on you, shoved you down and broke your ankle, and three days ago she poured Coke on your head?"

"She didn't shove me down or break my ankle," Langston barked. "I tripped and fell. I sprained my ankle. She didn't have anything to do with that."

"Still, though." Lucas pursed his lips. "Why would she get mad and dump Coke on you because you wanted to help her?" His eyebrows pulled together. "What exactly did you say?"

"I told her I would pay back the money she stole. That's it." Langston shrugged his shoulders. "Then she blew up and stormed off."

"So, she did steal the money?"

"Yeah." Langston ran his hand along his chin. "I mean, I'm assuming she did. Mrs. Landry said she did, and she wouldn't lie about something like that."

"I think I'm starting to get the picture." Lucas sat up straighter in his chair. "What would you say if Mrs. Landry ever accused me of stealing money?"

"That's ridiculous." Langston's eyes narrowed. "You're not a . . ." The words died on his lips and a look of dawning flashed in his eyes. He sighed. "She probably hates my guts."

"Probably."

A knock sounded at the door and both men looked as Mrs. Dean poked in her head. "Sorry to interrupt, but there's a man here with some boxes for you. He said his sister is returning your things?"

"That must be Fiona's brother. Send him in." Mrs. Dean closed the door, and Langston blew out another sigh. "It's probably for the best, anyway. I need to forget I ever met Fiona Madison."

A light rap sounded at the door again. A tall man with wavy brown hair walked through, his arms full of pale pink boxes. He stepped into the room, and Lucas rose, taking three of the five boxes from his arms.

"Set them over there," Langston said, pointing to an empty chair in the corner of his office. He walked around his desk and waited while the man unloaded his arms. The man wore faded blue jeans spotted with numerous grease stains, and a faded denim shirt with the sleeves rolled up to his elbows. "You must be Sidney." The resemblance between Fiona and this man was uncanny.

"Yes. Sidney Madison. Fiona's big brother." The man turned and stuck out his hand. "She said to bring these things by here." He tilted his head slightly to the side and glanced toward Lucas, then back at Langston. "She said to tell you the, uh, other box isn't ready yet."

"I'm really sorry about what I said to Fiona," Langston said, shaking the man's hand. "I wish she would just keep all of this. It's hers anyway." He looked over at the boxes and then down at Sidney's hand. "Sorry, didn't mean to shake your arm off. Can you tell your sister to keep the," he paused and glanced at Lucas, who watched with an amused smile. "She can keep the other box of things, and you can take these boxes back, too."

"Look, Mr. Wade."

"Langston, call me Langston."

"Okay, uh, Langston." Sidney pulled his hand back to his side. "I don't know what you said to my sister, but I don't think I've ever seen her as mad as she was the other night when I got home from work. If it's all the same to you, I'm just going to stay out of this. If you want to talk to her, feel free. Whatever happened between you and my sister needs to stay between you and my sister."

"She didn't tell you why she quit?"

"She called you a—and these are her words, mind you, not mine, a bull-headed donkey who doesn't know his head from a hole in the ground." He chuckled softly. "When she gets hot under the collar, she can spit out words faster than most people can listen."

"Yes." Langston smiled at the soft-spoken man in front of him. "Yes, I imagine she can." He glanced over at the boxes and back at Sidney. "You want to sit down for a minute?"

"No. I've got to get going." Sidney nodded at Langston, then Lucas. "Fiona didn't do what the mayor's wife said she did. She is as honest as the day is long. If that's what all of this is about, then you are in the wrong."

"Yes." Langston mumbled. "I am." He watched as the man disappeared through the door, then turned and walked back behind his desk. "I guess that's that." He fell into the chair; shoulders slumped. "I don't think it would bother me so much if she didn't think I was a," he smiled sadly and looked over at Lucas, "a bull-headed donkey."

"Bro, in this case, I believe the shoe fits."

"I know." Langston sat up and tugged at his collar. "You should see how hard she works. She works circles around most of the men I know, including you."

"Why don't you give her a call?"

"No. I'm sure she won't speak to me, and I don't really blame her." He ran his hand through the top of his hair and pulled his chair closer to his desk. "I need to get my mind back in the game. I've been too distracted since she started working for me."

"What are you going to do about her quitting?" Lucas stepped over to the desk and sat down. "Is Mrs. Butler coming back soon?"

"No, I don't know when she'll be back. I might try to do everything at the house myself."

"Yeah, right."

"You lived by yourself for years without any help." Langston glared across the desk at his little brother. "I think I'm as smart as you are."

"I'm what Vivian likes to call low maintenance." Lucas tilted his nose down and waved his finger at his brother's suit. "I don't think anyone has ever said the same thing about you."

"Get to work or leave, Lucas." Langston hit a key on his computer and looked at the screen. "We've wasted enough time talking about me and my love life already."

"I don't know why you want to go scrub toilets and mop floors over at that enormous church." Callie clipped the plastic end off of her tubed popsicle and pushed the tip of the frozen purple Kool-aid to the top. "You couldn't pay me enough money to clean public toilets."

"I don't want to clean toilets any more than you do." Fiona picked up the sliver of plastic Callie laid on their gold and green flecked kitchen counter and tossed it in the trash under the sink. "When you become an adult, you do a lot of things you don't want to do." She leaned her hip on the edge of the cabinet and looked down her nose at her little sister. "It's about time you started acting a little more like an adult yourself."

"I'm an adult." Callie bit the end of the popsicle off and smiled at Fiona with purple stained lips. "But I still won't be scrubbing public toilets."

"You better be thankful Mrs. Ross was nice enough to help me get the janitorial job at the Presbyterian church. Scrubbing toilets is paying your Beta Club trip dues." Fiona leaned over and took a bite from the popsicle. "It's only temporary while May Jones is out having her baby. Mrs. Ross said when people see that the church trusts me enough to work there, other people will realize this thing with the mayor is all a big misunderstanding." She ran her tongue over her cold, sticky upper lip. "I sure hope she's right."

"I don't know why you don't just go back over to Langston Wade's house and apologize for going all crazy on him and pouring Coke on his head." Callie pushed more of the purple popsicle up from the plastic and bit it off. "It sounds to me like the guy wanted to do you a favor, and you got all goodie two-shoes on him."

Fiona pulled in a deep breath of air and looked out the kitchen window. The grass needed mowing. Maybe pushing the mower would work off some of the nervous energy she couldn't seem to get rid of lately. "I'm not going back to work for someone who thinks I'm a thief."

"Even if he doesn't care whether or not you're a thief?" Callie pulled the last bit of the purple ice from the plastic. "You have that rich guy wrapped around your finger and you're too dumb to see it." She dropped the sticky popsicle wrapper on the counter by Fiona's arm and walked out the back, the screen door slamming behind her.

"Langston Wade isn't wrapped around anybody's anything," Fiona yelled to Callie's back. She picked up the plastic and tossed it in the trash. "He's just a nice guy who's as dumb as a fencepost," she whispered. "His head's so big he can't tote it through the front door."

Fiona swatted a mosquito buzzing near her head and looked around the yard. She stretched her shoulders back to ease the muscles, careful to keep the push mower handle engaged. If the engine died, she didn't have the energy to pull on the chord to crank the thing again. Her neck and shoulders already ached from the hour of shoving the mower through the knee-deep grass in the front. The back would have to wait for another day.

She looked over at the decades old Cadillac parked on the side of the house, the grass so tall you almost couldn't see the hubcaps. Sidney promised to move the thing a month ago, yet there it sat. She leaned forward and pushed the lawn mower in the old clunker's direction, ignoring the burning in her shoulders. Might as well get it done. The yard looked like a junkyard, but at least it could look like a lived-in junk yard.

The soft rumble of a truck engine coming down the street

caught her attention over the buzz of the lawn mower. They didn't get a lot of traffic this far out of town. It didn't sound like the rattling old pickup their neighbor drove. The truck slowed as it came into sight and Fiona closed her eyes. Why was *he* driving down *her* road? *Please don't stop. Please don't stop.* She turned her back and shoved the mower around the corner of the house with a vengeance.

Fiona held her breath. The truck tires crunched on the muddy gravel drive. The engine stopped, and a door slammed shut. She pulled the lawn mower backwards, rearing the body of the mower up on the back wheels. Fine. Let him stop. She had grass to mow. Some people didn't have time to roam up and down the streets in their shiny double-cab truck. She pushed the mower forward on the back wheels and set the spinning blades down on the foot-tall fire ant bed nestled in the overgrown grass near the back of the Cadillac.

"Oh, great." Orange dust flew up from the ground. The ancient lawn mower coughed and sputtered in protest before throwing in the towel and dying. Fiona jerked the dead, useless mower back, sweat dripping off her nose. "Ouch!" She reached down and slapped at a fire ant, digging into the flesh on top of her big toe.

"You really shouldn't mow the grass in flip-flops."

"I mow in flip-flops all the time." Fiona winced and swiped another fire ant from her other foot. She stepped away from the lawn mower and the fire ants, toward Langston. He stood in the overgrown grass looking ridiculous in his two-thousand-dollar suit. "Sometimes I mow bare foot too."

"Here." Langston stepped past Fiona and grabbed the mower handle, pulling it back toward the front yard and the freshly mowed grass. "I can mow that for you while you doctor those ant bites."

"No." Fiona followed beside him. She grabbed the tail of her faded tee-shirt with Darth Vader eating a bowl of Cheerios on the front and wiped the sweat from her eyes. "I'm fine."

"Your face is beet red." Langston lifted his hand toward the hair sticking to the side of her cheek. He looked at her raised eyebrows and lowered his hand back to his side. "You should probably get something to drink and take a break."

"Langston." Fiona pulled a deep breath of air through pursed lips and blew it out slowly. "Why are you here?"

"You, um." He reached into his pants pocket and pulled out a gauzy floral scarf. "I found this in one of the bathrooms this afternoon." He held out the small piece of material to Fiona. "I know you like to wear it in your hair."

Fiona reached for the scarf. Langston's fingertips raked across her palm as he placed it in her hand. A pleasant tingling sensation lingered from his touch and sent a quiver to her insides. She pulled her hand away and looked down at the scarf. "Thank you." She stared at her hands. If she looked up, she might . . . regret what she had said to him before. She stared down, the silence forming a wall between them.

"I guess I'd better go."

Fiona listened to the truck door opening a few seconds later. She slowly lifted her chin and watched as Langston backed out of her drive. A shaking started in her chest. A tear splattered down on her hand, and she turned and stomped around to the side of the house. She climbed on top of the trunk of the Cadillac and lay back against the back glass. *I am right. He called me a thief. I am right to be mad at him. No matter how bad it hurts.*

CHAPTER EIGHTEEN

a chill crept down Fiona's back. She looked across the neat desk at Trina, the director of nurses. *Why does she keep her office so cold?* "When did she make this will?"

"Let's see." Trina looked through a brown folder with Catherine Fiona Madison typed on the front. "She filled out the first living will years ago when she and your grandfather were seeing Dr. Gand." Trina flipped another page. "It looks like she updated it again about five years ago, and then you two signed this one on her behalf when you placed her in memory care."

Fiona looked at the name on the folder, Trina's words running in circles in her head. *Nana's name is Fiona? How come she never told me that?* "We signed so many papers that day. I don't remember signing a living will." She glanced over at Sidney, his faced masked in calm absorption. "Do you?"

"Yeah. The social worker said if we wanted to change our minds about it later, we could."

"Oh." Fiona ripped the damp tissue in her hands, her fingers refusing to stay still. "If you say so." She swallowed the block of panic in her voice. "There's really nothing else to do? No medicine or drip or anything?"

"I wish there was." Trina's voice softened, her sad eyes watching Fiona. "If we send her over to the hospital, they can pump fluids into her. If that is what you want to do, that is perfectly fine. We can sign a new living will that says you want to take those measures."

"Will it help her?" Sidney asked.

"It may for a few days." Trina looked at Sidney. "But her body is so weak. It's possible it could swell her up. Make her more short of breath. With her mind and body the way they are, she will be back in the same shape she's in right now very soon either way. She's at a point where nothing is going to have a long-term positive impact on her health. The short-term impact could go either way."

"If we don't do anything though, won't it mean we are giving up?" Fiona dabbed the useless tissue to the corner of her eye. "Like we don't love her?"

"No, not at all." Trina pulled a fresh tissue from the box on her desk and passed it across to Fiona. "It means that you have looked at the situation, looked at your grandmother's expressed wishes, and you are honoring her by doing what she wanted."

"But won't we just be *letting* her die?" The words shuddered from Fiona's throat.

"Fiona, are you a Christian?"

Fiona's eyes narrowed, and she looked at the nurse. "Yes . . . at least I think I am. I go to church and pray and stuff." She tried to swallow again, but her mouth was full of dust, her throat refusing to cooperate. "Wouldn't this living will thing be a sin? I mean, aren't we supposed to try to help the ones we love, not let them . . . die?"

"The Bible teaches us throughout it that God knows exactly when we are going to die, even before we're born."

Trina's eyes crinkled into a soft smile. "Your grandmother is a Godly woman. Before the Alzheimer's got so bad, I loved to listen to her pray and quote Scripture. Even when she couldn't remember where her room was, she could say the twenty-third Psalm. The Lord is going to take her home when it's her time, not a minute sooner, and not a minute later. We would never do anything to try to speed this up, but we realize there's nothing we can do to stop the inevitable as well."

"Our job then." Sidney's deep voice pulled Fiona's head toward his face. "Is to take care of her the best we can while she is here." He reached over and took Fiona's hand. "We need to do what Nana said she wanted." He looked at Trina and nodded. "What do we need to do now?"

"I'm going to have a hospice nurse come talk to you." Trina closed the brown folder and looked at Sidney, then Fiona. "They'll make sure your grandmother spends whatever time she has left as comfortable as possible. We can move a cot in the room with her, too. You can come visit her any time, day or night for as long as you want." The phone on Trina's desk buzzed, and she stopped and answered it. "Excuse me for just a second," she said, placing the receiver back in the cradle. "I will be right back."

"Are we doing the right thing?" Fiona wiped the end of her nose with the tissue and looked at Sidney.

"I think so, Fi." Sidney squeezed her hand. "Nana is ready to go be with Jesus. I believe that with all my heart. Let's love on her as best we can until she's gone."

"I feel—I don't know." Fiona leaned her head over onto Sidney's shoulder. "Like I've failed her or something."

"Nana's dying has nothing to do with you." Sidney rested his chin on top of Fiona's head. "I know you like to keep everything in control, but this is something you have to accept."

Fiona sniffed and lifted her head. "Did you know Nana's name was Fiona?"

"No." Sidney's mouth turned up at the corners. "It's fitting though. You act just like her."

"Thanks." Fiona swallowed, her throat starting to work like it should again. "I'm trying to keep things together, but I really don't know how she did it."

"You're doing fine, Sis. Just try to remember who's really in control."

"This is not necessary." Langston looked around his kitchen at the stack of paper plates and cups needing to go in the trash, empty cereal boxes and take out boxes sat crammed in an overflowing trash can in the middle of the floor. "Now that I'm buying paper plates, it's not that bad."

"I would hate to have seen it before," Mrs. Dean whispered, glancing at Vivian. "I'll take the kitchen. You see what the rest of the place looks like."

Langston followed Vivian back to the living room. Piles of unfolded laundry spilled from the leather sofa to the floor. Empty water bottles, Gatorade bottles, and soda bottles lay near the recliner. Empty and partially empty Styrofoam containers lay scattered along the hearth. "I'm planning on cleaning all this on Saturday. You really don't have to help. I don't know why Lucas sent you two over here."

"What's that spot on the floor?" Vivian pointed to a brown, sticky area on the rug in front of the recliner. She picked several tan hairs off of a couple of towels on the sofa and curled her lip. "Are you letting Lester lay on your clean clothes?"

"He followed me in last night after I fed him." Langston shrugged his shoulders. "I didn't have the heart to put him back out. He sat in my lap for a while, but he's so big that it got to where I couldn't breathe. I shoved him off, and I guess I didn't notice about the clothes."

"How long has it been since Fiona quit? Two weeks?" Vivian walked over to the hearth and started picking up empty boxes and bottles.

"Seventeen days." Langston rubbed his hand across his jawline. "You haven't bumped into her anywhere, have you? Is she doing okay?"

"We got a snow cone Saturday, and I talked to her for a while. She's working there." Vivian turned and rolled her eyes. "Honestly, Langston. She looks worse than you. When are you going to swallow your pride and tell her you're sorry?"

Langston tugged at the neck of his shirt, loosening his tie and sliding it off. Thank goodness the cleaners laundered his dress shirts. At least he could dress decently when he left the house. "How can I apologize when she won't speak to me? I went to her house a while back, and she would barely look at me, much less talk to me. I've left messages on her phone asking her to call." He tossed the tie on top of the pile of laundry and bent over to pick up a water bottle that had rolled near the sofa. "I felt at one time, she was feeling the same spark I was feeling. I was hoping she was anyway." He raised up and crunched the plastic bottle flat in his hand. "Now, I think it was all just me seeing what I wanted to see. I mean, if she cared for me, wouldn't she want to talk to me?" He looked at Vivian, his eyes clouded with pain and confusion.

"Don't give up on her, Lang." Vivian stepped over and took the water bottle from his hand. "She has a lot on her right now, and I think she's scared to open up, scared of being hurt again."

"I didn't mean to hurt her." Langston ran his hand through the top of his hair. "I should have known . . . I did know deep down that she wouldn't take that money. But all I was trying to tell her was that even if she did take it, I didn't care. I would stand by her. It just came out all wrong."

"Yeah, tact is not your strong suit."

"Why does everybody keep saying that?" Langston followed Vivian to the laundry room and watched her open the supply closet.

"Here." She nodded at a roll of black trash bags. "Get one of those and open it for me. It looks like we need to start by going room to room and getting all the trash out of your house." She raised an eyebrow and waited. Langston shook open the bag and held it open. She dumped in the armload of empty food and drink containers. "This place really is a pigsty."

"I know. I guess I've taken a lot of things for granted."

"Ya think?" Vivian turned and started back to the living room, trash bag in tow. "You're a smart guy, Lang, but you need to take a step back and realize a few things." She walked over to the hearth and picked up a Gatorade bottle. "Behind the costly designer suits and expensive house, you are a guy who likes to eat junk food and slob around with his dog." She turned and put her hand on her hip. "And there's nothing wrong with that. Nothing at all." She took a deep breath and picked up a rock-hard end of pizza from under a wadded-up napkin. "I can tell you these things because I used to be you, except I didn't have the money to pull it off the way you are doing." She dropped the trash in the bag. "I wasn't this big of a slob either." Vivian reached over and patted Langston's arm. "The people that really matter, they don't care about any of this stuff. They care about you, the real you. Maybe it's time you let your guard down and show them the real you."

"I will, but how do I get her to listen?"

"Use that big brain of yours." Vivian's eyes twinkled. "If you can't get in the front door, try the back door. Whatever you do, don't give up." She looked around the living room and rolled her eyes. "You've got to get yourself straightened out, or we are going to have to have some sort of intervention."

Langston shoved his hands in his pants pocket and pulled out his truck keys. "I hate to leave you to do all this, but I need to run an errand."

"Where are you going?"

"I think my truck needs a little body work done."

CHAPTER NINETEEN

angston's truck tires crunched through the thick gravel yard as he eased into the drive of the garage. Empty vehicles littered the area around the metal building, all waiting their turn to be worked on by the mechanics. Langston stepped out of his truck and walked toward Alan Jackson's voice, singing about marrying a waitress and not even knowing her name, booming from somewhere inside the open double garage doors. One car, a shiny red Mustang convertible, perched on a hydraulic lift high above the others below. A black sedan sat on the concrete slab beside the Mustang, a pair of legs stuck out from under it, the work boots tapping time to the rhythm of the music. The zzt zzt zzt of a power tool came from somewhere in the dark cavernous building out of sight. Langston ran his hand over the crease of his suit pants. Why hadn't he changed before coming here? Why did he always insist on dressing large and in charge?

"Can I help you?" A short round man wearing gray coveralls and a matching gray baseball cap stepped out of the tiny metal building beside the garage. His cheek protruded with an enormous wad of tobacco, giving him the appearance of chewing on a baseball. The man spat a stream of brown juice into the gravel near his feet, then grinned up at Langston. "Sure is a hot one we're having."

"I need to talk to Sidney Madison." Langston said, looking at the logo on the man's cap and then the coveralls. *Floyd's Garage and Body Shop. We Give Old Wrecks New Life.*

The man nodded and stepped toward the mouth of the garage a few feet away. "Sid." He yelled, then spat in the gravel again as the work boots rolled out from under a sedan. "Somebody's here to see you." The man turned and disappeared back into the little building with the neon OPEN sign shining bright orange in the window, not bothering to look back at Langston.

Sidney stood, wiping his hands on a grease stained rag. "Hey, Langston." He stepped out of the garage and blinked as his eyes adjusted from the shady garage to the bright summer sun bouncing off of the gravel. "What can I help you with?"

Langston stepped closer and stuck out his hand. "I need to talk to you for a minute," he said, raising his voice over the music.

Sidney shook his hand. "Hold on a second." He turned and poked his head in the little metal building, then walked back to Langston. "Let's go over here where we can understand each other without shouting."

Langston followed Sidney across the gravel to a large, sprawling oak tree near the street. They stepped into the shade, and Langston wiped a drop of sweat from his forehead. Children in a trailer park across the street squealed as they ran through a sprinkler in the dusty driveway. A woman with a very pregnant belly sat on the porch steps of a nearby trailer, looking at her cell phone. "I need to ask a favor." Langston said, turning his eyes back to Sidney.

"What can I do for you?" Sidney leaned against the trunk of the oak tree and pulled a stick of beef jerky from his pocket. "You want to know about Fiona?" He peeled the plastic away from the dried meat and a spicy aroma floated through the air. "She's seen better days."

"Yeah." Langston looked down at his shiny black dress shoes coated with red gravel dust. He looked back up. "So have I." He watched Sidney bite off a piece of the jerky, staring at him. "I really made a mess of everything between us, and was hoping you might help me make things right again."

"Uh huh." Sidney pulled another jerky stick from his coveralls' pocket. "Want one?"

"Thanks." Langston took the jerky and peeled back the plastic. He tore off a small piece with his front teeth and chewed. "I haven't had one of these since I was a kid. I forgot how good they are." He swallowed. "When that thing happened with the mayor's wife, I tried to talk to Fiona about it, but I made a mess of it. All I did was get her mad at me." He tore off a bigger bite and looked across the street. The pregnant woman stood, yelling at the kids, and turned off the water hose on the side of her trailer. "I've tried to talk to her, to explain myself, but..." He watched as the woman disappeared inside the trailer. One of the children, a little boy who looked to be around six, stepped over and turned the hose back on, restarting the sprinkler. He looked back at Sidney. "But she won't see me. I've tried to call her, but she won't take my calls."

"She definitely has not been her normal self. I'm sure some of it has to do with Nana dying, but."

"Your grandmother died?" Langston asked, cutting into Sidney's sentence. "I hadn't heard."

"No, she's still alive, but the hospice nurses are expecting her to go any day now." Sidney put the last bite of his jerky stick in his mouth. He wadded up the little piece of plastic and shoved it in his pocket. "I know Fi is having a hard time dealing with losing Nana, but even before that, she hasn't been herself. She's not a crier, but since you fired her, I hear her in her room at night boo-hooing."

"I didn't fire her." Langston rubbed the back of his neck. "I never had any intention of firing her. She just got mad and quit."

"That figures." Sidney pushed up off the oak tree. "Langston, Fi is not a hard woman to figure out. She likes pretty dresses and shoes just like most females, but that's not what makes her tick." He paused, wiping his greasy fingers from the jerky on his coveralls. "All she really wants to do is make ends meet in our family. She doesn't mind being poor." He looked across the street to the trailer park and grinned. The pregnant woman opened the door and yelled at the children, shewing them away to their own homes. She grabbed the little boy who turned the sprinkler back on and drug him inside. "Being poor is all we've ever known. What she can't seem to abide is people looking down on her because she's poor. I don't know exactly what you said to her on the day she quit, but if I had to guess, I would say you touched on her sore spot and she thought you were belittling her."

"I did more than touch on it." Langston's lips stretched into a thin line. "I punched it, shoved it, and stomped on it." He reached up and tugged at his shirt collar. "Do you have any idea what I can do to make it up to her? I'll do whatever it takes to make things right again."

"Do you really want to help her?"

"Yes. More than anything."

"Fiona needs her respect back. Right now, she feels like everyone in Carson's Bayou thinks she's a thief and a liar." Sidney looked back at the garage, then over to Langston. "If you really care about her, clear her name. Give her back her dignity." He patted Langston on the shoulder. "I hate to leave good company, but I need to get back to work."

"I appreciate your not being mad at me after what happened between me and your sister." Langston fell into step with Sidney, walking back toward the garage. "I'm a little curious, though. Why aren't you mad? I mean, your sister won't even speak to me."

"I look at it this way. Before you and Fi had your blow out, all I heard was Langston this, and Langston that. Even now, when Callie tries to say something against you, Fiona still defends you. I figure one day you two will get things right. Until you do, I am keeping my mouth shut."

Langston stuck out his hand and shook Sidney's again. "You're an alright man, Sidney Madison."

"Thank you. I try."

Fiona followed Mrs. Ross into the prayer room and looked around. Pastor Connors held open the door, and Mayor and Mrs. Landry stood near the stained-glass window with the hands folded in prayer across the room.

"Thank you for coming, Fiona." Pastor Connors closed the door behind Fiona. "If everyone will sit down, I'm sure this won't take long to sort out."

"I appreciate you and Mrs. Ross meeting with me," Fiona said, rubbing her hands together. "After our last meeting," Fiona looked across the room to Mrs. Landry, "I figured having a couple of people who believe what I say would be a good idea."

"Now, Fiona." Mayor Landry stretched his round cheeks into a taunt smile. "That's why I called you. Mrs. Landry and I know this is all just a big misunderstanding." He looked at

Mrs. Landry sitting beside him, staring ahead, back ramrod straight. "Right, dear," Mayor Landry said, voice suddenly firm.

"When I found the money missing after you cleaned the room, I logically assumed you took it." Mrs. Landry raised her chin and glanced over at her husband. "Since then, I've learned that my husband took the money and used it for . . . something else."

"See." Mayor Landry looked from his wife to Fiona. "See, just a misunderstanding."

"Wait." Fiona folded her arms across her chest, blinking slowly. "That's it?" She looked from Mayor Langston to Mrs. Ross and Pastor Connors. "She didn't even say she was sorry. And what does she mean, anyway? What's logical about thinking I'm a thief?"

"Fiona." Mrs. Ross reached over and rubbed Fiona's arm. "Let's give Mrs. Landry a chance to explain. Losing your temper won't help anyone." She turned and looked at Mrs. Landry. "Is there anything else you would like to add?"

Mrs. Landry looked straight ahead, eyes narrow. Mayor Landry elbowed her in the ribs. She grimaced and turned to Fiona. "I am sorry for what I said," she said, voice mechanical. "I did not mean to cause harm to your reputation. This has all been a misunderstanding, and I spoke out of turn."

Fiona looked at the couple. Mayor Landry fidgeting, his eyes pleading with Fiona to accept the apology, Mrs. Landry cold and uncaring. "Sure," she finally said, rolling her eyes. "Obviously, that's the best I'm going to get."

"You understand; however, that I can't hire you back," Mrs. Landry said, blinking her owl-like eyes at Fiona.

"And you understand that I will starve slap to death before I ever work for you again," Fiona said, her voice sticky sweet.

"Don't worry, Fiona." Mayor Landry stood, tugging his

wife up with him. "We will make sure the word gets around that you didn't do anything wrong, that this was all a big mistake." His voice took on its politician tone. "You can count on the Landrys to do the right thing."

"Yeah," Fiona mumbled under her breath. "Right." She watched as the mayor shook Mrs. Ross's and Pastor Connors's hands, then follow his wife out of the room. The door closed behind them, and she pulled in a deep breath of air. "I really am grateful to both of you for meeting with me today. When the mayor called this morning, I didn't know what to expect." She stood and looked at them both. "I'm just glad all of that is finally over."

"Fiona." Mrs. Ross reached up and took her hand. "Would you mind sitting back down for just a minute? I need to talk to you about one more thing before you go."

Fiona's eyes stretched wide, and she looked from her friend to her pastor. What in the world could possibly be wrong now?

CHAPTER TWENTY

"*M*rs. Ross." Fiona sat back in the chair beside the older lady. "I promise, I haven't done anything wrong." She wiped her sweaty palm on the side of her skirt. "I promise."

"No, honey." Mrs. Ross patted Fiona's hand. "I know you haven't. I've been praying for you ever since this whole money thing started and you came to me for help. I'm certain God has been working through all this, even if it's hard for us to see."

"I don't understand." Fiona's brow wrinkled. She looked at Pastor Conners sitting a couple of chairs away, then back to Mrs. Ross. "I appreciate your prayers, but you know I didn't cause any of this nonsense. What do you want to talk about?"

"You and I have chatted a lot lately." The wrinkles around Mrs. Ross's eyes deepened and her mouth turned up in a tender smile. "You've talked a lot about your grandmother and her faith in God, about going to church as a child, about worrying what your friends at church are saying about you." She reached over and wiped a brown curl from Fiona's eyes.

"But you never talk about Jesus, and how he is helping you get through this."

"Oh." Fiona slumped back in the chair, a sudden ache filling her chest. "I've tried several times to ask God for help. I really have." Her eyes darted to the preacher, then over to the window where the stained-glass hands waited, forever folded in prayer. "God just doesn't seem to be listening."

"Fiona." Pastor Connors stood and moved to the chair on her other side. "Do you understand what it means when you give your life to Christ? If you do, and He is your Father, I can promise you that He is hearing your prayers."

"I think I do. When I was six, I went down the aisle." Fiona twisted the tissue in her hands into a knotty strand. "I said that ABC prayer thing with my class at VBS, and a lot of us got baptized. Sidney too." She cut her eyes over to the pastor. "That was before you came here. I read my Sunday school lesson most weeks, and try to pray, but I just seem so . . . alone."

"Oh, sweetheart." Mrs. Ross leaned closer. "Giving your life to Jesus is so much more than saying something you memorized as a child. You have to surrender your will, give your life over to his control."

Fiona pulled in a deep, ragged breath, blowing it out through pursed lips. "I'm not sure God would want my life right now." She looked at Pastor Connors. "A verse you preached on a long time ago about filthy rags. I can't remember anything about it, but every time I really try to pray, that's all I can think about. That's what I feel like."

"I think God is speaking to you, Fiona." Pastor Connors said. "He's using that Bible verse to tell you to repent of your sins and give your life to him. Isaiah 64:6, is one of my favorites. It says that everyone of us is like filthy rags, no matter how many times we try to do good things. Our lives crumble like an autumn leaf, and our sins carry us away from God like a gust of wind."

"That's exactly how I feel." Fiona swallowed a sob. "It's like my whole life is crumbling. Everything I do is wrong. Almost everyone I thought I could trust has either let me down or..." A sob escaped her lips. "Or they have left me."

"People will always let us down." Mrs. Ross placed her hand on Fiona's back. "Even the ones who love us and mean well. They mess up. That verse applies to every person who has ever been born, except for Jesus. He's the only one we can always turn to, no matter what mess we find ourselves in."

"I don't understand why Jesus would want me." Fiona's eyes searched Mrs. Ross's face. "I'm so—broken, you know?"

"I think when we truly realize who God is, how great and perfect He is, we all feel that way." Pastor Connors nodded. "We realize how unworthy we are. But we are His creation. Even if we don't understand it all, we can love Him and become His child because He loved us first. We just have to give Him our life, every part of our life. He'll take our filthy rags and clean us up. You can give Him this anger you have toward the Landry's, and He will help you forgive them."

Pastor Connors leaned forward and looked into Fiona's down-turned eyes. "Believe me. If He could take the mess I made with my life and turn me around, He can do the same for you. You just have to surrender everything to Him."

"I need to do that." A tear dropped from Fiona's cheek and splashed on her hand. She lifted her head and looked at the praying hands in the window. "I'm not a Christian, but I want to be one. I need to pray. Get this right."

Mrs. Ross took one of Fiona's hand. "You can pray with us here, or we can leave you to pray on your own, whichever way is more comfortable for you. God is waiting to hear from you. I promise you that."

"Let me pray with y'all here." Fiona smiled and looked at Mrs. Ross. "I'm so grateful both of you are taking the time to talk with me." She turned tear-stained eyes to Pastor Connors. "I could tell I wasn't right, but I didn't understand why."

Pastor Connors took Fiona's other hand. "Just tell the Lord you recognize that you're a sinner. Tell Him you are sorry. Tell Him what's in your heart. You're ready to give Him your life, sins and all. You want Him to move in and take control. He will, and He won't let you down or leave you, Fiona, ever."

Callie sat in the old wooden kitchen chair, feet propped up on the counter, watching Fiona peel potatoes. "So, the old bird finally admitted that she was lying, and you didn't do anything wrong? It's about time." She stuck the diamond shaped purple ring-pop sucker in her mouth and pulled it back out slowly. "I hope you gave her and her hen-pecked husband a piece of your mind before you let them leave."

"I was mad at first." Fiona pulled the paring knife across the red potato skin peeling it away in curls. "But now I just feel sorry for them. Their marriage must be terrible. She tries to control him; he hides things from her. She always looks like she's eating a dill pickle, and he is always fake."

"I wonder what made her decide to come clean." Callie pressed her foot against the edge of the counter and leaned her chair onto its two back legs. "I bet Pastor Connors put in a good word for you or something."

"Maybe. I don't know." Fiona tossed the freshly peeled potato in the ancient aluminum colander and picked up another one. "I'm just glad that's over and done. Hopefully, by the time May Jones is done with maternity leave, I will have another job lined up."

"They didn't offer you your job back?" The chair plopped back on four legs, and Callie pulled her feet from the counter. "Figures." She stood and pulled the legs of her blue jean shorts down further on her thighs. "Oh, that hospice nurse called while you were gone. Said she couldn't get you on your cell phone."

"Callie." Fiona's brow pulled down over her eyes. "Why are you just now telling me? What did she say?"

"She said you need to go over to memory care today. Said Nana was changing." Callie stuck the sucker in her cheek. "It slipped my mind. What did she mean, changing?"

"Probably that Nana is not doing well, you doofus." Fiona dropped the paring knife in the sink and wiped her hands on a thread bare dish towel. "Did you tell Sidney?"

"No. You think I should?"

"Oh, never mind." Fiona grabbed her purse from the kitchen table. "Take the chicken out of the oven in thirty minutes. Don't forget. I'll be back later."

"Is Nana okay?" A sudden tremor touched Callie's voice. "Do I need to go too? Fiona— I haven't been to see Nana in over a month."

"No." Fiona turned away from the back door and hugged her sister. "No, stay here. I'll call you if you need to come." She pushed away and looked Callie in the eyes. "If Nana is dying." She paused, watching Callie's eyes stretch wide. "It is okay. She's ready to go to heaven. Right?"

"Yeah." Callie's lower lip trembled. "I love you, Fiona. Tell Nana I love her too."

"I will." Fiona turned toward the back door. "Don't forget to take out the chicken. I love you too."

Fiona leaned against the hospital bed and stroked Nana's pale forehead. "She's so cool." She touched her lips to her grandmother's sunken in cheek. "Love you, Catherine Fiona Madison. You know that? I'm going to miss you, but I'm gonna be okay now." She swallowed back the tears clogging her throat. "I met your best friend earlier this morning. He's my best friend now, too. When you are ready, you can go on home, okay?"

Fiona turned to the sound of a sob coming from the doorway. "Come here, Callie." She stretched her arm out in Callie's direction. "Come, tell Nana bye."

Callie walked over and scooted next to Fiona on the metal folding chair. "When Sid came back to get me, I knew it was bad." She sniffed and laid her head on Fiona's shoulder. "Can she hear us?"

"The nurse says she probably can." Fiona took Callie's hand touching it to Nana's face. "See, just Nana. She's getting ready to go, though, so you need to tell her goodbye."

Callie rubbed her hand against the old woman's tissue thin, wrinkled face, then laid her head over on her shoulder. "I'm gonna miss you so much, Nana. I love you."

Fiona rubbed slow circles on Callie's back. She listened to her little sister tell the only mother she'd ever known about what was going on in her life, rambling on, until she finally ran out of words. A hand squeezed Fiona's shoulder, and she looked up at Sidney, standing silently behind her. "We're going to be okay."

"We are." Sid wiped a tear from his cheek with the back of his hand. "You wouldn't have it any other way."

Fiona watched as the hospice nurse checked Nana. She glanced down at her phone. Six hours since she had hurried over to see Nana one last time. "She doesn't seem to be breathing, but I couldn't be sure."

"Are you here alone?" the nurse asked, keeping her voice soft and low. "Your grandmother just passed away."

"My brother took my little sister home a couple of hours ago, around ten." Fiona let the tears run down her cheeks, not trying to stop them. "Do I need to do something?"

"You can call your family, or anyone else that would want to say goodbye before we move her." The nurse gently wiped Nana's hair away from her forehead. "I'll take care of everything else."

"They said their goodbyes before they left." Fiona leaned over for the last time and kissed Nana's cheek. "She's in heaven now. I wondered why God let her linger so long, but I think I might now know." She stepped back away from the bed. The peace that filled her earlier continued to fill her heart. *I'm not alone. I'll never be alone again.*

CHAPTER TWENTY-ONE

*F*iona rubbed her hand up and down the arm of her black cardigan. Were funeral homes always this cold? It felt like a refrigerator in this place. She looked down at her long dark skirt, lingering on the black ankle boots peeking from under the hem. Quiet laughter tinkled from across the room, and Fiona slowly raised her head. Her little sister extracted herself from a group of her classmates and walked to where she stood at the foot of Nana's casket.

Callie looked so cute in her black fitted skirt and sleeveless matching top. She obviously wasn't cold. Her little sister floated through the sea of mourners like a young swan, naturally charming everyone with her smile and easy banter. Fiona smoothed her hand over the gauzy material of her skirt. She was no swan. Maybe a crow, watching everyone from a nearby perch. Not that it mattered. They were here to honor Nana.

Callie smiled and spoke to the different groups of people, young and old alike, huddled together in their private clusters, making her way across the room. Fiona slipped her hand in Callies when she finally drew near. "You did a good job picking out the flowers for the casket." She looked at the spray of white roses draping the dark mahogany lid. Three red rosebuds snuggled in the center of the sea of white petals, the contrast lovely. "Nana would love it."

"Fi." Callie squeezed Fiona's fingers like a vise. "I was wondering last night. Do you think our mother, our actual mother, might come? I mean." Callie's eyes darted around the softly lit room. "She could be here right now, and I wouldn't know it. I don't have a clue what she looks like."

"I guess it's possible." Fiona eased her fingers from her little sister's grip and slipped her arm around her shoulders. "I barely remember her. I probably wouldn't recognize her either."

Callie turned from the clusters of people and looked back at the closed casket. "I almost asked the lady to put a fourth red rose on for her . . . our mother, but it didn't feel right." She turned worried eyes to her sister. "I did right, didn't I?"

"You did perfect."

Callie took a deep breath and looked over at a ridiculously large wreath of lilies, roses, and mums, all soft white, with greenery weaving them together. "The mayor sent those. I guess that was nice of him, considering everything."

"Yes, very nice." Fiona stared at the wreath. "Kind of odd, but nice." A funeral worker stepped into the other side of the room with a stand of red roses and yellow sunflowers. "Look at those." She nudged her sister. "Those are gorgeous."

"I wonder who they're from." Callie took Fiona's hand and led her through the people to the other side of the room, nodding and smiling as she went.

"I wish I could talk to people the way you do," Fiona said when they reached the stand of flowers. "There's a lot of people here from the church and I see a couple of neighbors and some of the staff from memory care." Fiona's eyes trailed around the room, ebbing and flowing as people made their way in and out. "But there's a bunch of people here I don't recognize."

"You know how old people are." Callie followed her sister's gaze. "They go to church, to the doctor, and to funerals. Nana drug me to so many funerals over the years. I imagine a lot of these people are just returning the favor." She turned back to the flower stand. "Besides, Nana lived in Carson's Bayou her whole life. She probably knew a lot of people."

"I guess so." Fiona watched as Callie pulled the card from between a sunflower and a couple of roses. "Who are they from?"

"Langston Wade." Callie turned wide eyes to her sister. "Very nice. He came by the house again this morning while you were meeting with the preacher. Did I tell you?"

"No." Fiona pushed her lips into an annoyed frown. "You didn't. I promise, Callie. Sometimes you don't have the sense the good Lord gave a goose. What did he say?"

"He just asked if you were home." Callie sniffed the card and stuck it back in the spray of flowers. "I told him you were tying up some final things with the funeral. He said he would get with you later." Callie looked past Fiona to the doorway leading to the larger common room. "Speaking of." She nodded her head in that direction. "There he is. That man sure knows how to wear a suit."

Fiona turned toward the doorway, and her heart gave a lurch. Callie was right. Langston definitely knew how to wear a suit. Her eyes waiting, locked on his face as he scanned the room, waiting for him to find her. His gaze finally connected to hers. He strode over, people parting to let him through.

"I'm sorry about your grandmother," Langston said, eyes never leaving Fiona's face.

Fiona breathed in his clean, woodsy scent. "Thank you."

She searched his face, and a longing squeezed her chest. Giving her life to Christ, truly giving him her troubles, had made things better. Telling God how Langston's lack of belief in her had torn her apart had been so cathartic.

Now he stood in front of her, inches away, and a rush of feelings she thought she had under control coursed through her veins. The need to touch him raised her hand toward his arm, but common sense brought her hand back to her chest before they connected. "Thank you for the flowers." She tore her eyes away and nodded at the nearby stand. "They're lovely."

"I came by your house yesterday, and this morning. I needed to see . . . I wanted to check on you, but Callie said you weren't home."

"It's been kind of hectic." She smiled softly. His voice was so deep. Had it always been that deep? "I've been . . ."

"You have to be Catherine's granddaughter." A grey-haired woman wearing bright red lipstick, with a back so stooped that the top of her head didn't reach Fiona's shoulders, stepped up, wedging herself in front of Langston.

A rush of irritation washed over Fiona. She looked down at the intrusive little woman. "Yes, ma'am." She plastered a polite smile on her face, pushing the discontent away. "I'm Fiona, her oldest granddaughter."

"I'm Lillian Philmore. I was a friend of your grandmother years ago when we were young." Her pale green eyes traveled up and down Fiona's black ensemble. "You are the spitting image of your grandmother back before she was old."

"We don't have many pictures of Nana when she was young." Fiona's eyes darted back to Langston. He was still there. Of course, he was still there. Watching her. A warmth crept into her stomach, but the chattering woman took her hand, refusing to move on.

"Come over here with me and meet my husband," Mrs.

Philmore said, tugging Fiona away from where she desperately wanted to stay. "Just between you and me, my Bob was sweet on your grandmother before I came along and stole him away. He will get a kick out of seeing you. It's amazing how much you favor her."

Fiona looked over her shoulder at Langston, the woman steadily dragging her away. Her eyes captured his again, and he stepped in her direction, but stopped, his mouth downturned. The woman finally reached her destination, and Fiona stumbled into her back, righting herself before they both tumbled over. The woman's chatter was distant in her ears, but somehow, she said the right things as the group talked. The smile on her face remained, but the dark suit eased out of the doorway and a little piece of hope faded away, forever out of her reach.

"I don't understand." Fiona looked at the check for two thousand dollars, the funeral home director placed in her hand. "You have this left over from Nana's burial insurance?"

"Oh, no." The man looked down at his cluttered desk and shuffled through some papers. "It takes a couple of weeks for all the bills to come in. That's why I am just now contacting you with this reimbursement." He picked up another paper and ran his finger down the page. "Mrs. Madison's burial policy was only for five-hundred dollars. That insurance company hasn't even responded to our inquiry yet." He looked up from the paper, eyebrows raised. "I'm sure you realize that your grandmother's funeral costs were exceedingly more than five hundred dollars."

"No." Fiona leaned back against the chair, staring at the bald man. His pointed nose looked at odds with his round jowls, like he had forced a puzzle piece into the wrong space. "I didn't know how much her policy was for. I just assumed when we picked everything out, and you said the funds would cover our choices, that her insurance had paid up." She stared down at the check in her hand, her brow furrowed. "How can we have money left over if the policy didn't even cover the funeral? You're not making sense. Shouldn't I owe you money?"

"Let's see." The man turned back to the paper. "Here, see?" He turned the bill around and pointed to a section at the bottom of a long list of items she, Callie, and Sidney had picked out for their grandmother's funeral. "We received a cashier's check for twenty-five thousand dollars with instructions to cover the florist charge and any other super-fluous charges, no questions asked."

Fiona's mouth dropped open. "We spent twenty-three thousand dollars?" Heat crept up her neck. Her eyes scanned the charges. A thousand dollars for the casket spray. Ten thousand for the mahogany casket? "Why didn't you tell us how much we were spending?" The paper dropped from her fingers onto her lap. "I'm . . . I don't know what I am."

"The funds were there to cover your choices. I assumed that you would want the best of everything with that kind of money at your disposal."

Fiona's eyes narrowed. "Where, exactly, did this money come from? I'm sure you know it didn't come from me or my family."

"Well, no." The man shuffled some more papers, eyes darting around his desk. "The person specifically instructed me that this was to be an anonymous donation." He cleared his throat and slowly looked up at Fiona. "No names were to be mentioned to you, or anyone about this transaction, and any left-over funds were to be mailed to you. Since you came by to pick up the death certificate, I thought it would be alright to hand you the check." His fingers drummed across the top of his desk. "That may not have been a wise choice on my part."

"Who brought in the check?"

"I can't say."

"Man or woman?"

"Woman. Don't ask me anything else."

Fiona picked up the paper in her lap along with the check and rose from the chair. "The funeral was beautiful. Thank you for everything." She stared down at the man, her head tilted to the side. "I imagine what happened with our grandmother is an unusual situation, but for future reference." Fiona paused, choosing her words carefully. "Even when the bill is paid in full, most folks like to know how much things cost before they buy them. If they don't, they tend to feel a little hoodwinked."

Fiona stomped out of the funeral parlor and into the morning summer sun. How did she feel? How was she supposed to feel? Only one person could have done this. Is that why he had stopped by those two times before the funeral? Is that why she had not heard from him in the thirteen days since the funeral? She shoved the papers down into her purse and fished out her car keys.

It was time for all this cat and mouse, hide and seek nonsense to quit. She was a grown woman; he was a grown man. They needed to talk. This morning. She climbed into the car and started the engine. *First pray.* Yes, with the way this day was going, prayer was definitely needed.

CHAPTER TWENTY-TWO

*S*weat ran down Fiona's temple. Of all days for her little car to let her down, why today? The sputtering started right as she reached Langston's driveway to turn in. Shifting it into first to turn had been the straw that broke the Beetle's back. She had wheeled into the bottom of the drive with a hiss and a cough. She attempted to crank the engine several times, but the poor little car was not going anywhere until Sidney looked under its hood.

She should have just had Sidney come get the car and her, but she really wanted to get this business straightened out with Langston. She needed some answers before she saw her brother and explained to him why she had a check for two thousand dollars and a receipt for a funeral paid in full, not by Nana's burial insurance.

The trek up the hill was a hop and a skip in her little car, not so much on foot, especially in the mid-day summer sun. Fiona watched a yellow butterfly flitter across in front of her and land on one of the azalea bushes lining the long drive. She lifted her arm and took an unladylike sniff of her light blue baby doll tee-shirt. Not good. Oh well. He already thought she was a thief; a stinking thief wasn't that much worse. She walked across the circular drive and rang the doorbell.

"Fiona." Langston, face scruffy with what looked like a couple of days' worth of beard growth, stared at Fiona like she was an apparition. "What are you doing here?"

"We need to talk." Fiona's brow wrinkled. "Are you sick?"

"No." Langston glanced down at his bare feet, gray sweatpants with a mustard stain on the leg and the same tee-shirt he had worn for two days. "I'm on vacation." He stumbled to the side as Lester nuzzled past him and looked up at Fiona, wiggling from one end to the other.

"Hey, boy." Fiona squatted down in front of the mastiff and wrapped her arms around his neck, accepting his slobbery kisses. "I missed you too." She stood back up, holding Lester's collar to prevent him from getting loose in the front yard. "You sure you're okay?"

Langston stared at Fiona for a second longer. "Yeah. I just slept in this morning." He looked past her shoulder into his yard. "How did you get here?"

"My car is broken down at the bottom of your drive." Fiona jerked forward as Lester lunged toward an unseen enemy somewhere past the driveway. "Can we put him back inside, or in his yard? He's going to pull my arm off."

"Oh, uh." Langston frowned. "Sure. Lester. Sit."

Fiona looked from Langston to Lester, suddenly motionless, sitting at his master's feet, then back at Langston. "Has he always been able to do that?"

"Yeah." A faint twinkle appeared in Langston's eyes. "I kind of enjoyed watching you wrestle with him before."

"I bet." Fiona rolled her eyes. "Can I come in? We need to talk."

"Come on in." Langston pushed the door open. "I've got pizza. Have you had lunch?"

"No." Fiona followed him through the living room to the kitchen. "Pizza sounds good." She looked at the pizza box on the counter. A trash can set in the middle of the kitchen floor crammed to overflowing with empty Styrofoam containers and Gatorade bottles. "I see you haven't gotten a new house-keeper yet."

"Mrs. Butler will be back in two weeks." Langston pulled a couple of Styrofoam plates from an enormous stack by the sink and passed one to her. "Vivian and Mrs. Dean are helping me keep everything clean until she starts back."

"Oh." She put a slab of pizza on her plate and stepped over to the kitchen table. Lester lay on the floor under the table, head resting on his paws. She stepped back over to the counter and put two slices on another plate. She sat at the table and waited while Langston got a Gatorade and Coke out of the fridge. "I need to talk to you about something."

"Can we pray first?" Langston sat in the chair and slid the Coke in her direction. "Then we can eat and talk at the same time."

"Sure." Fiona bowed her head.

"Lord, I've made a mess of things."

Fiona raised her head and stared at Langston's bowed head. He sounded so— broken. She slowly dropped her head again, listening to his heartfelt voice.

"I've let my arrogance and pride cloud my judgement. I've let my stubbornness keep me from doing what I should. Lord, I know you've forgiven me, because you promise to forgive your children when we ask, and you never break a promise. Please Lord . . . please help me find the words to help Fiona see my heart. And thank you for this pizza. Amen."

Fiona raised her eyes and looked into his. "I didn't steal that money."

"I know."

"Then why did you say I didn't have to do that kind of thing? That you understood?" Fiona pulled in a deep breath. "I thought you knew me better than that. It hurt so bad."

"I made a mess of things." Langston's voice was flat, hopeless. "I never meant to hurt you. Fiona, I've never been in your situation. I've never had to make something out of nothing. Take any job I could get my hands on, and work all day for such a small amount of money. If I had, maybe I would have understood you sooner."

"What do you mean?"

"I mean, I." Langston paused and looked out the kitchen window. "I mean, I thought that because you are poor, and needed the money so desperately, maybe you did take it." He turned his eyes back to hers. "Now I understand that stealing would be impossible for you. I knew that then, I think, deep inside, but don't you see?" His eyes searched her face, desperation in his voice. "I didn't care what you had done or not done. It didn't matter to me then, or now. I *love* you. That love doesn't care who you are or what you've done."

"Like filthy rags," Fiona mumbled.

"Like what?" Langston leaned into the table. "What did you say?"

"It just dawned on me." Fiona bit her bottom lip and looked down. Lester shifted on the floor and laid his head across her flip-flops. "Christ loved me when I was in my filthy rags, when I was guilty of." She swallowed and forced her lips into a shaky smile. "I was guilty, and he loved me anyway. He didn't care. You didn't care either."

Langston reached across the table and stroked Fiona's cheek with the palm of his hand. "I hadn't thought about it like that. All I know is that I never should have assumed you took that money simply because you are poor, or that you would even want me to bail you out. I was such a." His eyes glimmered with a smile. "A bull-headed donkey."

"Maybe just a little bull-headed." Fiona leaned her cheek into his hand, her smile widening. "Definitely a little bull-headed."

"I should have looked into what happened with Mayor Langston. I should have talked to you and helped you figure things out. Instead, I waited until you were working your fingers to the bone at that church."

"Wait." Fiona's hand reached up and covered Langston's. Her eyes narrowed as things suddenly made sense. "Did you talk to the mayor? Is that why he made Mrs. Landry admit what really happened?"

"After my brother helped me see what an idiot I was being, and then your brother helped me see what an idiot I was being."

"Wait, you talked to Sidney?"

"I really like your brother." Langston pulled his hand back and scooted his chair closer to hers. "After that, I talked with the mayor. I told him how much honesty and integrity meant to me and that it meant even more to you. Since I have a lot of financial influence around town, he decided he'd better make things right."

"That's why he was so fidgety that day," Fiona said, eyes narrowed. "And that big ole wreath at Nana's funeral. No wonder he was making nice with me." She reached her hands out, taking one of Langston's large hands in both of hers. "I know what you did for Nana."

"Not for Nana." Langston leaned in, his lips so near Fiona's that she could feel his breath on hers. "Only for you."

"For me." She tilted her head closer, her lips barely touching his.

"Always for you."

Fiona felt his lips press against hers, but all thought left her as the rightness, the perfection of his kiss touched her heart.

EPILOGUE

"Do you really like it?" Langston looked down at the three-carat diamond surrounded by smaller rubies in the black velvet box. "If you don't, we can go get another one."

"I love it." Fiona rubbed her finger over the engagement ring and turned her eyes back to Langston. "You know people are gonna talk. We've only been dating for four months."

"So. Do you care?"

"Not a bit, but I do not have a business reputation that I have to be concerned about in this town either." Fiona stood on her tiptoes and brushed a light kiss across Langston's lips as the fireworks exploded in the twilight sky above the lake.

"My business reputation is just fine. Don't you worry." He sat their picnic basket on the grass and watched as she spread the blanket down for them to sit on. His khaki pants and polo shirt were starting to feel more natural than they had when he first started venturing out and about in something besides a suit.

The Carson's Bayou Gators, the high school band, began

to play a mixture of zydeco tunes along with patriot songs to celebrate Founders Day. A hint of fall cooled the air, but as expected, it was still perfect weather for a picnic, and most of the town gathered in the park to celebrate.

"Look." Fiona nodded across the grassy area to a man with brown curly hair much like her own. "Who is that woman Sidney's talking to?"

"I don't know." Langston sat on the blanket and pulled Fiona down beside him. "Listen, before my brother and Vivian get here and start trying to tell us what we need to do, I want to talk to you about the wedding. We can make it as big or as little as you want. I only ask one thing."

"What's that?" Fiona laid her head against Langston's shoulder and watched as he slipped the ring on her finger.

"I don't care how much it costs to make it happen, but let's make the wedding happen soon. I don't want to wait six months or a year."

"What if I do?" Fiona stared out across the park, biting her lip, keeping her head down so Langston couldn't see the grin turning up the corners of her mouth.

"Well, I guess." Langston looked down and put his finger under Fiona's chin, lifting her face up. "I guess I will have to be so charming and handsome that you will have to change your mind."

"Oh . . . well." Fiona's words were cut off as Langston leaned forward and kissed her. "Any time is fine with me." She breathed as he pulled back and looked into her eyes. "Any time at all."

Sidney flipped the switch on the wall and looked around the cavernous garage with the concrete floors, hydraulic lift, tire storage racks, and enormous toolboxes. It was finally his. Well, his and the bank's. He had been working and putting back for so long to own his own business. It was a little hard to believe the dream was finally coming true. A slow, mellow smile crept across his face. It had been worth the wait.

Fiona married in the spring, leaving him and Callie in Nana's old house. The old home place was literally falling down around their ears. It had been a pain trying to make sure Callie had enough of everything she needed for all of her high school clubs, sports, and activities, but it had paid off in the end. Callie didn't love math like Fiona, nor was she valedictorian like her sister, but she was a talker and could sell ice cubes to an Eskimo. In the end, the volleyball scholarship, along with the other smaller scholarships from the different clubs and activities, had allowed his baby sister to start college right on schedule this fall and pay for room and board at the dorms.

He walked to the back of the garage and opened the door

to the tiny office. A rackety old wooden desk took up most of the room along with a tall gray filing cabinet. The computer set alone on the desk, waiting to be put to work. The bare sheetrock walls would probably remain bare, except for a possible calendar, but Sidney didn't plan on spending a lot of time in the little office, anyway. He had a good head for business. He and Fiona had that in common, but where Fiona thrived on figures and balancing the books, he loathed the whole process. No, he would eventually have to hire a secretary, and she could do what she wanted with the office walls. He planned on spending his days in the garage.

Honk honk. Sidney closed the office door and hurried across the garage and out the side door to the gravel parking lot. He didn't officially open until tomorrow, but already had several jobs lined up. Maybe somebody saw his truck out front and decided to drop their vehicle by a day early.

"I thought we would find you here." Fiona Wade, Sidney's younger sister by eleven months, stepped out of the passenger's side of the shiny black Tahoe. "Have you started moving in yet?" She looked at the metal stairs going up the side of the building leading to the little one-bedroom apartment above the garage. "We figured you might need some help to get your mattress and bed frame up those stairs."

Sidney looked over his shoulder to his future home. The studio apartment had seemed like a great idea when he was building the garage. He had planned to move in yesterday, but for some reason, the idea of leaving the family home, the place he had lived since he was five years old, brought on an unexpected wave of, what . . . nostalgia? "Yeah, I guess getting that old dresser and bed up there might be a two-person job. There's no hurry, though. I can do it a little along if I have to, and just keep staying at the old house until it's done."

"While we're here, let's go ahead and get a load and bring it over," Fiona said, pushing her chestnut colored braid over her shoulder. "I want to see where you plan on putting everything."

"She's been rushing to get over here ever since we left church this afternoon," Langston, Fiona's husband said. "She's really just being nosy and wants to arrange your furniture and stuff for you."

"That's right," Fiona said, raising an eyebrow. "He's my only brother and needs my help. If I don't help you." Fiona turned from her husband to Sidney and smiled. "You know you will keep everything shoved together and in boxes for the next five years."

Sidney patted his jeans pocket. "You're probably right." He pulled out the keys to his red double-cab Ford pickup. "Let's go load a few things."

"We don't have to if you don't want to, though." Fiona said, pulling on the handle of the Tahoe. "I don't want to be pushy or anything."

"Hmph," Langston snorted, "I think your brother knows you better than that."

"Hush Lang," Fiona said, glancing from her husband to her brother. "Until we find him a wife, I have to make sure he's taken care of."

Dream on, Sis. Sidney chuckled as he climbed into the cab of his truck, listening to his sister- and brother-in-law swap words. They were so good for each other. Fiona could be as hard-headed as a slab of granite. From an early age, she learned that as long as pain wasn't involved, Sidney pretty much let her do what she wanted where he was concerned. Things ran smoother that way, and it saved him a lot of arguing, which he liked to avoid, anyway.

Langston didn't seem to be bothered by her need to run things, but he didn't mind drawing a line in the sand when he felt it was necessary. Sidney had seen the man put his foot down a few times since they had married. It was kind of weird. Fiona had some kind of sixth sense and knew when she couldn't win an argument. She didn't bother fussing with Langston when that happened. She wasn't that way with Sidney; however.

Sidney pulled out of the parking lot onto the street and looked in his rearview mirror. Fiona was leaning across the seat, holding Langston's face in her hands as he tried to drive, planting kisses on his cheeks. Having someone in his life like that would have been nice. That melancholy feeling settled on his shoulders again. What was wrong with him today? He wasn't the type of guy that dwelled on things he couldn't have. That type of dreaming was a waste of time.

He looked out the windshield at the orange and red leaves on the oak trees as he drove through town. The concrete statue of Carson the alligator, the town's mascot, stretched across the front lawn of the bank where Sidney had gotten his loan for his business. Soon the town's folk would decorate the statue for Thanksgiving, and then Christmas. The kids around town loved to get their pictures made with the concrete mascot over the holidays. He sighed and turned his eyes back to the road.

No, family life wasn't in God's plans for him. If his business did as well as he projected it would, he could get the garage paid off in half the time of the loan contract. Then what? He stared out the windshield, driving without really seeing, and braked at the last stop sign before turning toward the street leading out of town to his old run-down house. He looked out his side window. A woman around his age stood in her little yard, raking leaves. A toddler played nearby on a blanket with a cat teasing the curly-headed child with its tail. How did that happen? A guy just found the right girl, and he knew she was the one? Then they got married and made a family? It was all such a big gamble. What if she wasn't the one? How did they know?

When Fiona started working for Langston, did she know he was the one? For a while, they acted like they were going their separate ways, but somehow, they had worked everything out and turned into the happy couple in the Tahoe behind him. He wouldn't ask his sister these kinds of questions. If he did, she would start trying to fix him up again. If he let her do that he would go out with a girl and do something stupid, and mess everything up and be embarrassed, just like all the other times. No, whatever everybody else seemed to have, that thing that let them know they had met *the one. He* didn't have it. That had become obvious. Best to stick to the role the Lord had laid out before him, friend and brother.

He slowed his truck and dodged a particularly nasty pothole. The roads got a lot rougher toward his home, but so did the houses. He pulled into the muddy dirt driveway in front of the ancient house he grew up in and watched as Fiona and Langston pulled in beside him.

"Sidney, you really need to mow." Fiona lifted the hem of her long gypsy skirt and waded through the sea of knee-high grass to the front porch. "I guess I can come by one day this week after I'm done with my classes and do it for you."

"No." Langston put a hand on Fiona's shoulder and stepped up the sagging porch step behind her. "You can't. And don't be picking up on anything heavy today or I will shut down this little moving venture so fast it will make your head spin."

Sidney watched Fiona reach up and get the house key from the rotting frame above the front door. "We don't have to do this today if you're under the weather Fi. I can stay here just as easily as I can stay across town."

"I'm not under the weather," Fiona said, shoving open the front door. It creaked as it scraped across the old hardwood floor. "We never did get around to fixing those hinges, did we? I don't guess it matters now."

Sidney followed Fiona and Langston into the living room, flipping on the light switch. A basket of clean clothes sat on the couch from where he had been to the laundry mat yesterday, and there was a layer of dust on the TV, but overall the place was fairly neat, unlike the yard. "Y'all want a Coke or some tea?" Sidney asked, stepping around Langston, who had stopped in front of the old brown velvet couch with the wagon wheel arm rests. "I will have to borrow a dolly before we try to move the fridge or the dresser, but I think we can get the bed frame and mattresses."

"I'll take a water." Fiona opened the olive-green fridge and handed Sidney a Coke. "I don't want the baby to have the caffeine."

"Baby?" Sidney looked at Fiona and then back at Langston.

"Yes, brother-in-law," Langston said, the smile so wide it probably made his cheeks hurt. "I'm going to be a father. You're going to be an uncle."

ACKNOWLEDGMENTS

Thank you to my wonderful readers who encourage me and lift me up in prayer as I try to make my stories come to life, be entertaining, and shine the light of Christ through my characters and the struggles they are going through.

Thank you to my beta readers who hang with me every time I hand them a story and ask, "what did you think of this one?"

Thank you to my group of writer friends. You know who you are. I message you telling you I'm not sure I can write another word and you nurse me through until the story straightens itself out again.

Thank you to my family who frequently move my laptop off the kitchen bar, the living room couch, out of the recliner, wherever Mawmaw happens to be writing when you drop in.

Thank you, Mr. Wonderful. You keep my men manly; help patch up the plot holes, tell me one more time to break up the run on sentences, and give me hugs when I'm just completely wore slap out.

Thank you, Father for letting me do what I love and reminding me why I write.

A LITTLE ABOUT KC

KC Hart is the author of inspirational romance and humorous southern cozy mysteries with a Christian world view. KC lives in Mississippi with Mr. Wonderful, her husband of thirty-eight years, where she spends her days enjoying the grandkids, reading, writing, and playing her piano or guitar. One of her favorite things to do is sit on the back porch in the evening and eat watermelon before the mosquitos come out to play.

You can follow KC at her webpage and sign up for her monthly newsletter:

kchartauthor.com.

Amazon:

www.amazon.com/author/kchartauthor

Book Bub:

https://www.bookbub.com/profile/kc-hart?list=author_books

Good Reads:

https://www.goodreads.com/author/show/20570083.K_C_Hart

A NOTE FROM KC

Dear Friends,

I wanted to let you know how much I appreciate the support you show me through the emails, social media posts, cards and letters. I have come to know so many of you through this type of contact and you have made my life richer.

I ask, as always, that you continue to pray for me as I write my stories. I am always reading books on how to improve my writing, but the one thing that is most important to me is to share the heart of Christ correctly and in a meaningful way to the reader. I feel this type of evangelism is what my writing is all about. I want my characters to pull people closer to the Lord with their stories and I want my stories to get into the hands of those that will enjoy them and those that need to see them. Again, thank you for all you do.

Blessings,
KC Hart

Made in the USA
Columbia, SC
02 April 2022

58407534R00098